To Anthony & Anne with

ISLAND SOUPS AND MOROCCAN BEACHES

hosts of thoughts over past years
Comrade friend & mentor.

Geoff 5-11-08.

Also by Geoff Broady:

Lovers of the Planet Unite (poetry anthology)
Earth First or High-Tech Disasters

Island Soups
and Moroccan
Beaches

Geoff Broady

UNITED WRITERS
Cornwall

UNITED WRITERS PUBLICATIONS LTD
Ailsa, Castle Gate, Penzance, Cornwall.

British Library Cataloguing in Publication Data:
A catalogue record for this book is
available from the British Library.

ISBN 9781852001346

Printed in Great Britain by
United Writers Publications Ltd
Cornwall.

To all freethinkers,
anarchists, spiritual vagrants,
nonconformists and
lovers of the planet.

Contents

1

Devil Rock
(A robbery in Morocco)

1

The winter tides rolled in with unusual fury during the month of January, 1973, on a stretch of the Moroccan-coast about nine miles north of Agadir, and Tom felt alone and unwanted as he watched Devil Rock being pounded by the Atlantic. The proud defiance of the outcrop of volcanic stone, as it resisted the swirling thud thud thud of the angry waves, gave him courage as he walked past it covered in mist and spray. Devil Rock seemed so steadfast amidst the ever-changing scene: as though put there by a divine providence to remind the forgetful that the solid constructions of nature endure, whereas the puny efforts of men fall into the abyss and are lost forever.

Tom enjoyed the company of Jerry Crossland, an ex-patriot teacher and his young French boyfriend Paul. They had exchanged poems, cooked special dishes and swam together for about two months. Then Tom remembered how Jerry had felt when his young friend left him. He took a trip to Tan Tan in the south of the country, "just for a change of scenery," he'd said, and meanwhile Jerry's health suffered as he'd cut his ankle on a jagged piece of coral whilst bathing, because of neglect. It went septic. Tom had taken him to the hospital with a terribly swollen leg and high fever and they had to wait three hours before Jerry was treated.

Now Jerry and Paul had gone off together, once more united in a deep friendship; down south, through the deserted areas of Morocco and Mauritania into Senegal.

Tom privately wondered whether the old Bedford Dormobile-van would make the trip: but that was their concern; he had his own problems vis-à-vis his passport visa expiring in a couple of weeks or so: and where to go then?

If only he felt more secure inside. Why was he so sentimental about friends? Now he had a few new friends: Ian Campbell and his wife Ann and their charming young daughter Betty. Yes, they were good, reliable people: but they weren't interested in poetry and they didn't swim much. They were eminently much better than the others though. Those weird hippies who smoked kif all day and had such loose undisciplined habits and who held midnight gatherings in the big bell-tent, sited to the left of Devil Rock, on the sandy escarpment above the lovely sweep of wild, untamed beach, that received the uncertain affections of the uncontrollable Atlantic. What had got into these hippies? Something of the primitive spirit of Nature herself supporting their barbaric form of life!

Anyway, the dogs were a comfort.

Especially Rasputin, who enjoyed life so much and who spent every day as though it was his last and when the sun set, he nearly always found another dog, or if very lucky, another bitch to celebrate the days' dying. Then there was Lady, his natural half-sister, whom he treated with the greatest respect. A well-bred desert-dog: amber coloured, medium sized and a nose that could smell a ripe 'bit of leftover fish, or a high piece of meat, from a distance of about two kilometres.

The Campbells didn't like the dogs urinating on the edge of their tent, which they found they could do, without losing their doggy dignity; but Ian and Ann were happy to find that Tom's doggy-friends, guarded the camp at night and barked viciously whenever marauding Arabs came snooping around at night to see what they could steal. And when the little girl went off, to do something privately, the two dogs accompanied her for safety and her Mummy had told her not to be embarrassed by their presence, as their instincts were strictly honourable.

"Well, Lady, there's no bones for you here my girl: only wet old sand and an empty beach. Where's that rascal Rasputin? Come on! Let's go back, we've walked far enough. She sniffed around the rocks as they returned past Devil Rock, and came running at full-speed with a piece of dead-fish dropped by one of the Arab-vendors who had been unable to sell all that day. "Ah, here's Rasputin! And how's Betty today?"

"I've had a swim and the water was so strong it nearly pulled me under."

"Yes, the winter-tides are very strong: you must take care! Did your Daddy go in with you?"

"Yes, but he only paddled a bit. Mummy asked me to tell you to come for supper at about seven."

"Oh, that is nice! It's about six now, so I'll just feed the dogs and see if the wind-wheel is producing any current and then I'll be along. Tell your daddy I'll bring a bottle of Moroccan red wine if it is suitable to go with the meal."

Tom had made an electricity producing wind-wheel from scrap-material from the sea and a generator, lifted from a burnt out Jaguar remains that had served as a cheap but uncomfortable place for poverty-stricken hippies to sleep in, on the island of Las Palmas, near the docks. He was very proud of this very pure machine, for it had been constructed lovingly from pieces of drift-wood etc., and when the wind blew strong enough, it charged his car battery: free of charge.

An American television company, whilst making a documentary-film about Morocco, had been intrigued by the assortment of European holiday-makers, camped freely, on the coast and had taken a film of all the weirdies.

American draft-dodgers and other respectable, if somewhat adventurous folk, who preferred to camp by the sea: if only to get away for a short spell from the cluttered and encompassed lives that they have to live whilst in the cities.

Tom had explained that the name of his doodle was 'Phoenix' and that he was interested in 'Ecology'. He thought that modern rationalisation-techniques of production were highly extravagant of world-resources and that soon disaster would come upon those who design obsolescence into their products! The director thanked him profusely, but gave him no money for the filming and spoken description of how it had been made: so Tom was a little out-of-countenance with the profit motive, and industry and commerce generally.

Bread, milk and some left-over potatoes from lunch had to do for the dogs, together with whatever else they could catch from the motley gathering of humanity. The wind was slackening now, so no charge on the volt-meter. It had to revolve at nine hundred revs to be effective: requiring a ratio of about twelve to one on the gear-system. Anyway that was that and now for supper.

The Campbell's convertible Volkswagen was very comfortable inside and as there was a large fitted tent at the entrance Ann had plenty of space to do her family chores, and Betty was a great asset, helping her father: especially on barbecue-nights, when she liked to skewer the little pieces of mutton interspaced with onions and tomatoes to make a delicious shish kebab over the charcoal grill: and she often did the washing-up for Mummy too.

"Just fit yourself in on that side Tom and we'll try your wine. It should be OK! I've had it in the fridge since Betty brought it over and it will go with meat."

"Oh, it's great to eat in a civilised manner for a change, Ian, you don't know how much I appreciate your invitation."

"Think nothing of it Tom! It's a change for us too. I know the wife so well I can even hear her thoughts, especially when she's in a bad mood: like just now, for instance, she's thinking that I'm neglecting her, talking to you and drinking without her."

"I can hear every word you say and if I have any more of your sauce I'll pour this hot soup down your trousers."

2

It was a delicious meal, and after Ann tucked her daughter up, all had a good natter. Ian had been a flying-officer during the war and could talk well on most subjects until they began to discuss the present hippie-scene. "I don't know much about them but it seems to me that their brains are in third-gear and their exhaust-pipes in first-gear." (Ian put it a little blunter than this.)

"Could you make just one good flying-officer out of the lot?" Tom asked, with heavy irony, tinged with contempt in his voice.

"No, definitely not, but of course they are mostly untried youngsters: green as grass and still wet-behind-the-ears. Better give them a chance to enjoy their fling: life is serious enough and it will catch up with them. Their reality is the dreams they dream, ours are the hard facts-of-life: which aren't too rosy these days for any of us."

"Anyway, I suppose we'll both find out more about them tomorrow. Tracy, the tall-boy, who went with us to the bank earlier today, has invited us to supper: but because of convenience, they are having their supper in two separate tents and so you've been invited to one and me to the other, smaller one."

"Oh, that will be a chance to get away from the wife for one evening at least. We've been spliced for ten years and she's wearing me out."

"Don't think I'm not listening to every word you say, you traitor: you wait till I get you in bed tonight, we'll see who's the boss! Now come on you two, you'll have to chew the cud outside under the stars, for I want to convert the van for sleeping. That's if there'll be any sleep for us with all this infernal 'music' from three pop-cassettes going at once!"

"Oh, how I agree with you Ann! They do have poor taste, when it's always *Deep Purple* or Dylan all the time. Just to hear a Beethoven piano concerto for a change would be Heaven!"

Tom and Ian took a walk and Tom fastened up his trailer for the night and all turned in.

The following morning clear skies and a hot sun didn't tempt all into the sea, quite a number sat loafing around: smoking hasheesh almost till lunch-time. Tom made a strong stool out of bamboo-canes, which grew plentifully, acting as a windbreak just beyond the farmer's fields, which were without shelter and only used for poor pasturage for the goats and a few sheep that often found it more profitable to eat the garbage from the careless tourists, who threw everything onto the sandy-ground, sun-burnt and unburied: so orange-peels, banana-skins and bits of paper were eagerly consumed by the hungry beasts. The stool was a success: as he found it useful to get up onto the top of the van and also as a small-table for afternoon aperitifs.

Night fell, ushering in a full-moon and an extremely clear, starlit sky, and delicious smells assailed Tom's nose as he trimmed the vanes of the machine. The wind was freshening, so he made the most of it but couldn't resist looking expectantly in the direction of the smallish red-coloured tent where he was due to eat soon. Ian had been busy repairing a small car bought by Tracy from an Arab in the nearby village of Tarasute for the princely sum of two hundred and eighty dirhams (about twenty-eight pounds). A. broken cylinder-head bolt had not helped matters and so the two men had been obliged to pool resources in order to fix it up. Ann and her daughter had a paddle and did some rock climbing, until the wind got up and nearly blew them off Devil-Rock into the sea.

Tom bought some doughnuts off a couple of young Arab boys, late afternoon, hopeful that they would stay fresh when he wished to present them to those in the tent. And now there were some swarthy, evil-faced Arabs on bicycles, stopping off at various tents and vans along the sandy track. "Ah," thought Tom, "the old Arabs selling their rubbish to the unsuspecting young again: Silly buggers! Got more money than sense! I wouldn't trust an Arab to cook my dinner, let alone sell me some evil old mixture which they dignify with the dubious name of Kif." Which seemed to Tom to mean 'marijuana' or 'hasheesh' mixed with any old

15

rubbish to make it go further. He felt a kind of wild, furious indignation welling up inside him, to see the young being so easily duped by these foxy 'sons of Allah'. Good British youngsters and a few clean-cut Yankees, frittering their health and their birthright away, in an artificial dreamland of expensive make-believe: and when they come down, all the problems previously confronting them are still there but they usually grow into unsolvable ones, and so the vicious spiral begins and ends with them being completely broken in health and destitute of all worldly goods. Well, he couldn't stop them. Impotent fury was of little use and only reduced one's own vitality, so his thoughts turned hopefully to the evening's pleasures.

Just before supper, Ian and Tom dug a deep hole in the ground: not too far away, for Ann to empty the garbage without inconvenience and so the sand could be shoved in to bury it, keeping their patch at least sweet and clean. Ann didn't want anyone in her family to go down with a fever whilst on holiday. They had already had major repair to the engine and being canny Scots they didn't wish to spend any more on doctor's fees: apart from the dangers of cholera which was a killer!

"Well, enjoy your supper Ian! See you in the morning all being well!" As an afterthought, he said, "How's Ann and Betty?"

"They're fine thanks! She's a bit upset at being left alone: but she's made a cold salad for supper and she's reading Ernest Hemingway's *Death in the Afternoon*, so her mind will be filled with the romance of bull-fighting and Spanish 'Amar' (Love). I'm expecting our love-life to take on new dimensions of passion after she's finished reading it. Cheers. Have a good time!"

Ian put on a pair of light slacks and a clean shirt, grabbed his last bottle of Johnny Walker and strode across. He was no ballet-dancer in build, he was built for heavy-duty, like a coal-barge, rather than an elegant-schooner, so he had difficulty making it inside the tent. He was a man of intelligent clean-cut features, with a worldly-wise look on his eager, open face: that is, what you could see of it, for the bottom-half was somewhat obscured by an auburn-coloured curly beard, which gave emphasis to his eyes, which in turn danced with good-vitality. Just now, however, he wore a petulant disturbed look upon his normally serene brow. He wasn't quite sure as to what the results would be of his visit to this crowded tent. Some 'flying-instinct' told him that all was not quite as it should be: but he brushed these doubts aside, as Tracy greeted him and accepted the gift of whisky.

Tracy beckoned him to a space upon the roughly-carpeted floor. Inside it was hot and oppressive so he took a glass of lemonade and a cake, like everyone else in the party. There were about ten hippies dressed in an assortment of Arab djellabas, thobes and burnooses: necks and wrists garlanded with leather thongs, from which were suspended colourful Goulimime beads. Hair was very long, unkempt and greasy. He ate the cake, just like any other home-made bun and thought no more about it. Then the talk was about flying and his exploits during the last war, which the present company seemed to enjoy: for he was an expert raconteur; liberally spicing his descriptions of flying in to home-base in foggy weather: the plane badly holed from flack, half a wing shot off and the Krauts eating sauerkraut out of British Tommies helmets when they flew in to bomb their trenches. Then sailing and the joys of escaping from all formal social-systems of life whilst trusting one's fortunes to the billowy depths. This was followed in due course as the 'stuff' got moving along the blood, with the discussion of women in general and women's lib in particular, and Ian was 'agin it' for he didn't hold with truculent, unmanageable wives, nor did he hold with loose unmarried women, who would open their legs to any man. His whole life had been fairly disciplined and he was basically very contented with the results. Now, though, he was feeling distinctly uneasy: queasy in the stomach. He didn't know it at the time; but the 'stuff' was depressing the higher centres of consciousness and self-control: releasing him into he knew not where, except that right now nothing seemed to matter any more: wife and child receded into nothingness.

Two hours later, Ian lurched into his van to be greeted by exclamations of disgust from his young wife. "What on earth is the matter with you?" she said with an alert but disgusted look upon her normally happy face. "Come on, let me put you to bed, you look quite sick!"

"I'll be OK, but I don't know what those 'baskets' gave me in those 'cakes' that they were handing out. Oh, I do feel queer! Give me a glass of water Ann."

Meanwhile, it's a full-moon outside and a cloudless sky, and Devil Rock is sustaining the pounding of the Atlantic as usual. Tom was eating supper in the red tent unaware of what was happening to his friend Ian: but he was in a funny state also, having gone out once to vomit. Tom had mixed feelings about trusting his sensitive stomach to the culinary efforts of these people: but what with swapping paperbacks with one pretty young wife and helping to fix the car, his instinct to want to join in and be sociable had won the day.

At last all slept; the cool and the stoned: the alert young wife, sleeping now close to her husband, as if to guard him from further harm, and their innocent daughter: all asleep, but no! Stealthily, alert as hell itself; keyed up and steeled ready for danger, a thief approaches Tom's car. No one knows whether he's European, American, Moroccan or African. The door is opened expertly the first time with the right key. The two guard-dogs are asleep, inside the tent with Tom: Probably they've been doped too. Tom's sleeping soundly, completely out. The courtesy-light is deftly removed from inside the car. With the aid of a narrow-beamed pencil-torch, the thief removes Tom's bankroll; electric-shaver; gas-cylinder; cooker harmonica-recorder (his only form of musical joy), food and clothes. All are professionally stowed into a sack: the door is closed to but not shut and the bandit disappears into the Muslim night.

The next morning Tom was rudely awakened by the sonorous call of the matowas calling the faithful to the mosques for early prayers. He looked out onto a blissfully calm day, with the waters just idly lapping the beach with gentle love-pats. He noticed a yellow sock hanging down from the left-hand side-door of his car and was immediately alert. "I don't remember leaving the car door unlocked," he said to himself. "What in the name of all suffering humanity has happened to me now?" Only the previous day he'd stocked up with food, got everything ready for the long trip back to Ceuta, in the north, and then this to happen to him of all people. He examined the car, found out the extent of the rip-off, started up and went to the Policia Royale in Agadir: gave a full account of the theft, which was duly typed up and promptly forgotten about. "Sign here please," the police clerk requested. "Good morning, sir." And that, he supposed, was that.

3

Tom returned quickly to the beach, to warn Ian of the dangers of camping upon open ground. "Take care Ian, you know you've got a lot of stuff in your trailer and it's only covered with a canvas sheet. The 'baskets' might get you next time."

"They already have, Tom! I feel shattered! It's now eleven o'clock and if it hadn't been for the wife, I think I should have died last night and I wouldn't have got up at all. But she told me of your bad luck and gave me strong coffee because I wanted to speak with you when you returned from the police."

Tom thought, yes, he does look bleary-eyed and a bit vacant: but he didn't feel too good himself either after eating in the tent from that great big stewpot, in the middle of the dark interior of the tent, on that fateful last night.

Anyway, Tom could see the sympathy growing in Ian's eyes as he outlined his destitute state. "The mother fertilisers!" he exploded. "They don't deserve any quarter shown to them if they are discovered."

"Well, come on now, tell me your story. What happened to you last night?"

"Tom, the point of attraction in life can so quickly turn into the point of departure," he said profoundly. "Just let anyone offer me, my wife, or daughter a cake like the ones that they gave me last night and I swear upon everything that I hold sacred in life, that I won't be responsible for the consequences. I felt like dying, Tom, and that's the truth!"

Just then the dogs came up. It was feeding time but Tom had no food to give them. After half an hour, Ian came over and handed Tom one hundred dirhams. "Here, this will help tide you over until your money comes through from the bank."

"Thanks a lot, Ian. It's a great help! Now I can eat today."

"Think nothing of it, Tom! I know you'd do the same for me if I'd been done over instead of you."

The robbery brought the two men very close and Tom ate many times with them, eating the most delicious meals prepared by Ann and her daughter. The feast of Eid (the festival of the Arabic Muslim New Year) was upon them and the Arab world went mad: as the Christian World goes mad in the New Year celebrations. Tom telexed for money but it didn't come through. Still no reply on the twenty-seventh of January. The police were difficult about extending Tom's visa because he had no visible means of support. The Phoenix machine was revolving idly in the breeze, until Tom took it up, stowed it on the roof of his car, said his fond farewells to the Campbell family and entered the official campsite for security. Tom tried to persuade Ian to do the same, but he loved the sea-coast too much and said he'd take a chance. Rasputin was sad and Lady no longer lived for she'd been murdered by thieves about three days after the theft; for her constant habit of barking at the Arabs as they passed by. Ian's holiday with his family was partially ruined, ironically enough, for his genuine attempt to meet the youngsters halfway. The whole family gave Tom love, hope and money in his desperate hour of need. Tom bought an Arabic-style tagine charcoal stove, made from clay, and lived very simply, until his money arrived safely. Then he said good-bye to all his true friends. Ian lingered on, at odds with the rest of the hippy crowd.

They continued as before.

Devil Rock stood quietly by, smiling a timeless grin at human folly. It had seen it all before so many times. What the rock didn't require for itself, it had given to the greedy sea, its 'eternal mistress', before a thief could steal it. The rock stood defiant and alone, but triumphant.

2

A Gift from Allah

In the closely woven carpet of Moroccan life there are vivid contrasts of light and shade. Bold primary colours competing with tinted shadows making bolder still the clear designs of Muslim life in schools, mosques, casbahs, shops and boudoirs.

Mustapha Haffiz had lunched with his wife and four sons and took up his new beautifully bound Koran from pride of place, set on the cedarwood desk in the corner of the guest-room, and ordered his sons to listen to his reading of the second book of suras. They sat dutifully enough, cross-legged in front of their austere father, upon a new Isfahan carpet Mustapha bought off an Iranian pilgrim during his own visit to Mecca five months ago.

His solemn dignified voice impressed the boys more than the text. There was such conviction and strength in his tones. Only Rashid, his eldest, fidgeted uneasily, his eyes down-cast as he contemplated the delicate shades of mauve and yellow that seemed to challenge the classical blacks and whites in the intricate patterns below his shrouded legs. Was he perhaps a new scion growing from old roots? He felt confused, for only that morning the gymnastics teacher had insisted he change into vest and shorts. And yet here was his father reading and saying not to expose the body in the company of others, except for washing the five orifices before entering the mosque for morning prayers.

His revered father stopped reading and the sons departed and left him to rest until the evening, when he would serve in the shop. But before he settled to rest he motioned to Rashid.

"Rashid, go and clean up the floor of the shop. Sort through the fruits and vegetables, take care! Don't throw any out unless they are bad. Put the cakes on display under the glass-shelf to keep the flies off and put the fresh deliveries of bread in the bin. Then cut two hundred wrapping sheets for grain, spice and sweets, then you can amuse yourself for two hours before evening prayers. After that I want you in the shop with me to serve the tourists."

"Oh father, please let me go down to the beach and sell doughnuts and fresh bread to the tourists? You know I always make a good profit and I don't take long on my bicycle."

Mustapha hesitated, his thoughts racing, concerned for his eldest. Alert that he could get into bad company, or worse still become too friendly with the infidels and Kafirs, who were good for business but whose lax way of life, called 'life-styles', threatened the whole of the Muslim faith.

Young men dressed in very short shorts and no shirt, flaunting themselves, their money, cars, badly behaved children and their half-naked women.

"Oh very well, take the remainder of this morning's bread, together with a dozen fresh ones, taking care to mix them, and two score doughnuts and be here at sunset."

"Thank you, Father."

"And Rashid, you can keep twenty-per-cent plus any tips if you return empty. Remember to always offer your best smiles to the wives or girlfriends of the howajhas. They love Arab boys more than their own. But do it when the men are not looking."

"I know, Father, I've learnt that trick from Ahmed. He does it when selling fish for his father."

"Right, and don't forget, two dirhams for four doughnuts. Not as in the shop, five for two, and one dirham seventy-five for each loaf and come down to one-fifty if they are awkward."

"Agreed Father, I'll clean the shop first."

Mustapha mused dreamily to himself about providing and being a strong example of Muslim culture to his family so as to help them resist the snares of easy material pleasures paraded by rich Europeans flooding in during autumn until late spring. They ate pigs, drank wine, beer, spirits and worshipped a strange god and motorcars. Furthermore they cooked in aluminium pots instead of good earthenware Arabic tagine stoves, so economic with a little charcoal. They wore machine-made clothes, loved dogs and showed too much false sentiment for friends and relatives, but who demonstrated no love for Allah, and therefore little genuine love for each other.

"The boy is intelligent. He will learn to discriminate. Not to judge everything by its appearance and price but by its intrinsic value. Allah will guide his steps as he guides mine."

He recollected his wild days as a goatherd shepherd for his father up there in a remote mountain village in the high Atlas. How proudly and how fervently came the hope that his sons would maintain that dignity and fortitude of mountain-life down here on the coast close to lush pastures, watered and made fertile by peasants who respected the cascading rivers which carried the rich alluvium, essential for the good crops, including citruses and bananas.

Mountain-folk they were, driven there in the wars. Christian zealots against Muslim fanatics, in what was euphemistically the 'Crusades'. Called this quite wrongly in the West. We in Europe seemed to forget that under Saladin the great, the Muslim religion of Islam had once stretched from Spain to Turkey, on into Persia, Afghanistan, Pakistan and India, the Middle-East and North Africa.

In more recent times, French colonialists had tried to convert the Muslims to accept Christianity and modern ideas but had failed even after defeating them in battle. And now Mustapha felt himself to be something of a traitor to his own beloved faith and the sacred language of the prophet, pure Koranic Arabic. Is it not disgrace enough to speak a foreign tongue and to even have one's children corrupted by infidel habits, thoughts and science, taught in French to Arabs? And all this is assumed to be progressive and modern?

One day, he thought, the Arab world will wake up and reassert its ancient cultural values and dispense with cheap machine culture from the Western hemisphere which has caused so much confusion in Morocco, so much that even the butcher watches French trash on his Japanese screen. And now he talks of a wind-charger to charge his batteries instead of going to Agadir to do it, taking his mind off Allah. He dozed off into a troubled sleep where men turned into nightmare robots with no creative abilities and no hearts.

Rashid accidentally knocked the curry off the low shelf with the broom-handle and thanked Allah gratefully, for the tin landed on a large bag of couscous (semolina). The lid

25

b

sprung off, spilling some of the rich spice onto the small white grains so he grabbed the half-kilo wooden-scoop, hand-carved by his grand-father and carefully removed the coloured spice from the sack.

He finished his duties, drank a couple of Coca-Colas and trusted his judgement that his father wouldn't notice two extra empties.

"Always drink fresh orange or lemon-juice my son," he'd said, "because it is better than artificially produced soft drinks as they are made for profit, not for the lining of your stomach. Leave them for the stupid tourists who'll pay for any popular concoction, in dress, food or drink and begrudge paying one and a half dirhams for a whole kilo of fresh oranges."

His father wasn't always right and he liked to think he was doing something that the rich tourists did. He grabbed his bike after knocking a couple of chickens off the handlebars. They ran squawking across the courtyard where Ashara, his first dog, used to eke out chained up all day, until he stole meat whilst his mother was occupied in front and his father killed it with one blow of the cleaver. Poor 'Ashara', meaning 'ten' in Arabic, lived but two short years since Uncle Mohammed-Ali from Agadir gave the dog to him on the tenth day of the holy month of Ramadan, the Muslim month of fasting and reaffirmation of faith, between dawn and dusk.

At eight years he tried to fast like fourteen-year-olds but after three days of fasting he dozed off in class due to exhaustion, so Mum made breakfast as usual for him and, he remembered, she gave him one kebab sandwich and a glass of mint tea. Now he was a strong fourteen-year-old with wild mountain blood in his veins.

As he secured the bread-box onto the carrier of his bike

he thought of those happy days when he took Ashara down to the pier or the beach to watch the heavily laden boats when the fishermen would throw baskets of fish into capable hands.

Loaves went into one section and doughnuts into the other and the lid secured to stop the sun drying them too quickly. Then he went! What a friend his bicycle is, he thought. Freedom, mobility! And most of all adventure, getting away from the Alimentaires General store, his home and his family duties.

Hitching his djellaba under his belt to free his legs he was soon racing along the coast-road to the caravans and make-shift tents where the rich lived in style and the hippies in squalor. Freely encamped right on the cliff-edge where he often prayed to Allah.

This was his own spot for secrets to pass between himself and Allah. Resentment was in his heart but not showing on his face as he stopped at the first big caravan giving one of his seductive smiles to the fair haired smooth-faced lady at the door. " Salaam, salaam," he greeted but she eyed him with cold suspicion so he tried in French. "Bon jour madame! Gateau et pain, tres frais?" Still no response, so it must be English. "Fresh bread and doughnuts, plenty fresh with sugar and jam, special price for nice beautiful lady from London?"

She was delighted to hear him speak. A strong sexy voice emphasising the vowels so charmingly. "Just one moment, I'll ask my husband." She disappeared and this gave Rashid time to inspect the car and van. Two gas-cylinders under the trailer-bar and what looked like a refrigerator next to them, not even chained. Quite easy to take at night, for instance. Just then a tall hard-faced man pierced him penetratingly with cold blue eyes as he emerged so that his soul froze.

"Isn't he a pretty boy, Vibrant, with those black eyes and long lashes? He's good looking enough to be a girl. Let's buy two doughnuts for supper."

"Yes. He's nice looking but evil enough to be a thief more than likely. How much for two?"

Rashid pretended to struggle at these words, although he understood perfectly as he gazed admiringly and with great ardour, he addressed the lady. "Special price for English lady. "Four for two dirhams or each one for seventy-five centimes." This speech was effective.

"Go on Vibrant, buy four they are cheaper that way."

"OK, four at special price for my friends." He wrapped them gently in thin brown paper and handed them to her with grace and charm. "Very good business. See you tomorrow, salaam effendi."

Out of the car next to the caravan jumped a fine desert dog. It barked at him playfully whilst he wheeled his bicycle in between the blue Seat van and the Volkswagen variant. Why should such a strange old man, dressed in a white shirt and black shorts, possess such a fine desert-dog? he thought to himself. He's friendly now but he's a guard-dog at night, then he isn't so amiable. Rashid loved Sandy from that moment on and immediately felt like stealing it from the grey-haired frail old howajah. What right did he have to a free-born Moroccan desert-dog anyhow?

Eyeing him shrewdly, Rashid leaned his bicycle against a rock and asked, "Do you want fresh Moroccan bread?" Instinctively he knew this man to be well-travelled and as shrewd as himself. He had that same wise look of the religious teacher in his day-school. The price for him had better be one-fifty for bread and not to mention doughnuts, so he began beaming one of his irresistible smiles whilst caressing the dog's sandy-coloured head and ears, and

28

looking to see if they were out of ear-shot from the Dutch couple: "One-dirham-fifty for you, special price?"

The old man gasped in astonishment. "What! I'll give you two-forty for two and even at that, you're making a big profit."

He wrapped them carefully and handed them over reluctantly, making it a big effort to part with loaves at that price.

Whilst the man fidgeted in his purse to find exactly the correct change, against the possibility of Rashid cheating him, the lad saw the wide-open nostrils of the man's nose, the bulbous end, and mentally compared it to the finely chiselled nose of his father. No fine breeding in these strangers. Spawned in the materialist Western jungle. His father was right. They were the products of a machine-culture. Relating to machines and mass produced trivia in an intimate way and towards each other like stereotyped robots. There seemed to be no dignity in any transaction, let alone buying bread. No human dimension of knowing how difficult it is to sell bread in a hot climate. On and on his thoughts raced like a magistrate weighing the cultural pros and cons.

"Yes, they treat me like dirt. With all their cars and caravans they have no souls. Anyway, I have my bike and maybe I'll be rich and own a shiny car one day but right now I have a strong body and a perfectly shaped nose. And I've won prizes with my brass tea-tray made in the craft-room and on display in our guest-room. Yes, to be an Arab is the best fortune for young boys living a simple life under the will, the eternal will of Allah, which the prophet Mohammed had revealed to the faithful." He never left plastics, tins, domestic debris, littered on the otherwise unspoilt beaches as these tourists did. Encouraging rats to breed, then invade the coastal villages.

A plan formed in his swirling brain. "Steal the dog just to even the score with these sickly invaders from Christian shores . . . perhaps tonight when free from shop duties."

Yet another fellow stepped, like a ferret, out of the blue van into the fast dying sunlight, revealing a bald head, shrunken white legs and a fat paunch above faded red and white trunks. The skin of the stomach was covered with a thin blue vest. A flat spade-shaped face supporting a self-indulgent smile, hovered around the weak mouth. Fishy eyes looked at him with an intimate knowing look (as much as to infer that he knew all about Arab boys).

"Two doughnuts please, young man."

"OK sir, very good price for you . . . seventy-five centimes each, or four for two dirhams?"

"Two please, young man."

"Alright, one dirham fifty, OK? Allah cuum salaam." He stretched out to shake hands after handing the cakes and pocketing the money. The hand-shake was like grasping a cold cod-fish. He kissed the back of his hand to show respect but felt nothing, then placed it over his heart as if finding it a great effort to reverence ancient foreigners. He embraced the saddle of his bike affectionately, jumped on and was off.

Nearly time for prayers and no lamps or brakes so he whizzed past small tents and bamboo-huts where drop-outs lived, where the draft-dodgers and kif-smokers squatted. They never spent except on bare essentials and often went without bread.

He next tried at a big caravan with oval-shaped matricule from California, where he sold eight doughnuts and two loaves to a pretty young wife. Then there was the eucalyptus tree he'd climbed, at seven years, and years later he'd fastened his first mongrel desert-dog to that same tree whilst in the fishing-boat with friends. He'd shared that indefinable comradeship of danger in heavy seas when the whole catch, boat and crew, could have sunk.

A strong young man now, with fantasies of being a leader, like Saladin, to lead Muslims into battle against the howajas. But right now he was desperate to love something of his own. Normally Rashid wasn't an avaricious boy but that fine dog stuck in his mind. He'd be just right to guard the shop. And what aristocratic colours. A chosen dog! Free but not free! Owned by that strange man having a desert-dog for company in such a small car. "Yes, father is right. They are sentimental fools." He'd be useful as a guard and he'd take him on fishing-trips as with Ashara.

He raced until he saw Abdullah his school-friend and stopped to explain his plan to steal a dog from the infidels.

"Very well, I'll help and I'll be there at the corner, at nine tonight."

He counted the takings. His father gave him his commission then he went to wash and change before prayers.

He washed his genitals carefully after his father's admonition to be scrupulously clean before going to the mosque. He donned a clean grey camel-haired djellaba and said his prayers next to his friend Abdullah.

Freeing himself from shop-duties just before nine, he dashed to the corner of the main road, with a few scraps of meat stuffed into his large pocket and a length of rope from a packing case.

His father shouted, "Don't be more than half-an-hour as supper is nearly ready and your Uncle Khalid is eating with us tonight."

"OK. I'll soon be back," Allah had said nothing definite

about him stealing the dog so he assumed a clear conscience.

"Is that you Abdullah?" he asked darkly for his hood was up, and he looked along at the stream of foreign cars passing by.

"Salaam, Rashid."

"Come Abdullah, I have to hurry back soon."

The night was black. Scudding clouds obscured the stars. No moon tonight shone, as though the night was alive with a thousand evils. The sea moaned in mourning for human folly below the stark cliffs. The sparse looking eucalyptus branches bent in the wind as it gusted through the allotments where the locals grew their fruits and vegetables.

Both boys worked as one. Abdullah fell like a trained tumbler and Rashid stopped pedalling in the standing-up position and with an agile roll, shoved the bike into a clump of bushes on the allotments. They stole across the intervening sandy beach in bare-feet, making no sound and down wind wherever possible.

The Englishman was in earnest conversation with a Dutch couple. The dog rested near an almost burnt out barbecue fire. They hid behind what once was a coastal fort and threw a small chunk of meat near the unsuspecting animal. He sniffed then ate it and looked at the two, too late, for a noose dropped round his neck so tight it could make no sound. Between them they stole it away into the blackness. Gaining the bushes they eased the rope for it to breath freely giving Sandy more meat. Onto the bicycle once more and away with the dog loping contentedly at the side of the bike with Abdullah clasping the rope-end.

"Shukran Abdullah annah shuffak intah bukarah in challah." (Thank you Abdullah, I will see you tomorrow if it is the will of Allah.)

"Salaam, Rashid!"

After tying the dog to a stump let into the concreted yard, and stowing his bike in the shed, he went in for supper. He ate heartily and slept like an innocent.

Whilst breakfasting he explained to his father that a kind foreigner had given him a dog and could he please keep it? "Yes, but you must pay for its food or cadge scraps off the rich tourists when you sell bread."

"Very well, Father, I agree."

At geography lesson he shared sticky sweets, given by Uncle Khalid, with Abdullah, sitting next to him. They were sucking avidly on these stolen delights when Abdul-Ali looked up from marking books. "Rashid and Abdullah come out front. Eating sweets in class, eh? Hold out your hand Abdullah, swish swish . . . and now you Rashid. I'm surprised at you, swish swish . . . now, to your seats."

Their mutual present suffering and last night's escapade cemented them in a close comradeship which only Arab boys can do, for there are intricate spiritual movements within the severe frame of Muslim culture that cannot happen inside sophisticated industrial so-called 'Christian' cultures.

After school they both threw stones at a crazy old man who lifted his djellaba high above his crotch exposing that part for all to see. Then as they passed the butcher's shop an irate man caused a commotion outside it arguing with the butcher about the price for a notice to be displayed. It transpired that the Englishman offered a reward to anyone finding a sandy-bodied dog with white tips to tail, nose and paws.

Rashid went pale under his swarthy chocolate complexion, wondering, fearing that Abdullah might split on him. But no, he decided his friend was solid. The butcher left the notice up for twenty minutes, before deciding the dog-owner had had his five dirham's worth of publicity and with an inward smile then took it down.

Mustapha read to the family from the Koran as usual after lunching together. Instructing his sons that Allah expects every good Muslim to learn more every day of their lives. "To know is often better than to do. And to do on the basis of profound knowledge rather than hurried decisions without principle. Don't copy the ways of the infidels for they are without dignity and lack a sense of duty to Allah and to each other. One day I will take you my sons to Marrakesh and show you the arts and sciences of that city. When you achieve your Baccalaureate you will go to Fez University and I hope you will study to become religious teachers. You shall go to an Arab university, no more French studies, although it is important to know the language of enemies. Remember, ours is a human religion based on practical wisdom not a mechanical ideal. There is no art at the level of daily life to bind them together. It is bifurcated, where low people called 'workers' do all the dirty work and those climbing up the ladder, the clever ones, become separated from the dignity of everyday life and become fops and educated nincompoops unable to make things with their hands but simply design trivia and quite unnecessary gadgets assembled by idiots in mass-production factories. So there is a rift between designer and producer which results in machine-made goods, inartistic to look at or to handle. They live wretched soulless lives. Good money but cut off from all inspiration from Allah. Thus they become inhuman, a mere extension of the machines they buy and worship. We must be proud of our arts and our simple needs. Every year thousands die and others are injured and diseased from factory-pollution, motorcar crashes, petrol-refineries and chemical plants. They eat artificially refined and produced foods that are not good."

Rashid slept badly that night . . . heavy with a troubled conscience. What would his father think if he knew the truth? And what would the the dog-owner do if he got no results from the withdrawn notice?

At that moment, the crazy old dog-lover was in audience with the headman (Sheik) of the village, asking for his help. The old bearded wise-acre didn't dig why this fuss for a desert-dog should concern him, but he agreed to speak with the headmaster of the village lycée, "That's all he'll do," said the interpreter.

Sandy barked in response to the old man's whistle, for by now he was fed-up and wanted the freedom of the beach and tit-bits from the hippies, but he was secure inside a high-walled, Arab yard right opposite the butcher's shop

Should he take the dog to Agadir and give the unhappy animal to Uncle Ahmed? Ahmed, whom he loved as a brother, would care, until the hue and cry died down.

Today being Friday the Arabic Sabbath, he took Sandy off to Agadir, although he'd miss him as he had become so close to himself.

Still the man haunted the village every night whistling with renewed determination, when he discovered the butcher had foxed him.

Rashid hit on a plan that only a cruel Berber boy from the high Atlas mountains could form. Kill the beast and so destroy the evidence. It would be hard, for the animal was affectionate and he needed love. He told Ahmed his situation and he understood by permitting him to return Sandy to the village after only three days in Agadir. Rashid had cycled over frantically eager to put his plan to work. They returned . . . he on his bike and Sandy running home to his death.

At eight-o-clock, just as the fierce glow was setting, he took Sandy high up along the cliffs in the direction of Agadir. Exactly at sun-set he stopped for prayers, near his old eucalyptus tree, about a kilometre from the caravans.

The sun dipped suddenly and in so doing it cast a lurid glow over the beautiful coastline, somewhere along which Sandy had been born some two years gone.

After praying, ritualistically facing east towards Mecca, he looked to where he'd tied his loyal friend to a tree. The dog was at ease watching a lizard crawl towards him from its home in the sand under the rocks. The moment came for him to kill his friendly dog and all was quiet and still.

As he bared his long Arabian dagger from the folds of his robe, his mind was disturbed and his will faltered, for had not Allah reminded his conscience to love and forgive all living things? He approached the peaceful animal reluctantly. It jumped up and licked the hand that held the dagger.

Rashid, suddenly overcome with remorse tinged with self-pity, bent and released the dog. It gave a happy bark, sprang up and licked his face eagerly. They cuddled, then both strolled back at a leisurely pace to the shop.

At last they understood each other perfectly and are now true companions in the adventure of life for as long as they live. Nothing more was heard of the irate Englishman and for ever after, Sandy accompanied Rashid to his secret spot near the eucalyptus tree, to commune with Allah, 'the greatest and the most merciful'.

3

The Last Supper

1

"Well, what's your verdict? Is it worth the fifty dollars I gave for it?"

Andy listened carefully to the small Seat 600cc engine. The bonnet was up and Andy had fixed a couple of jump-leads to the dead battery to give her a start. Both men were examining the engine, as it coughed and sputtered at the back of the tiny saloon.

"Timing is all to cock and you've got water leaking from the cylinder-head gasket. Not surprising really, as there's one cylinder-head bolt missing altogether," replied Andy, with a nonchalant air of expert diagnosis in his strong voice.

Fred looked a trifle disappointed and wiped the perspiration from his boyish face with the back of his hand and dried it on the side if his bathing shorts.

Andy, who had served during the war as an RAF mechanic and who later qualified as a civil airlines pilot and who was presently on holiday with his wife Jean and daughter Linda switched off and said, "It all depends on whether we can fix a new bolt. Apart from that, I think you've got a bargain!"

The two friends walked over to Fred's old green ridge-tent, sited near to Andy's VW combie, and sat and drank a bottle of Moroccan wine between them, as they discussed the repair-job which Andy said would take about six hours to do. They looked out contentedly enough over the wild coastline, just beyond Tarasute near Agadir, in Morocco. "This is the life Andy. Much better than New York City: Or Vietnam, come to that."

"Yes, I agree, you meet all sorts out here. It's so different to flying: just booking in and out of the same hotels and eating at the airport-terminal restaurants so often. No chance to really meet and talk as you can here."

"It's cheap and easy with good bathing and quite a few chicks for a bit of sport now and again."

"I'm married! It's OK for you youngsters, coming here with plenty of time and money, wish I was thirty years younger. The war took up most of my early days in the love-stakes: sixty hours a week servicing Hurricanes and Spitfires."

"Well at least you didn't have to serve as a Marine in the American Navy and later in combat-duty, North of Saigon!"

"And now you don't believe in fighting any more?"

"That's right man! On my first leave back home, I burnt my draft-card and scarpered and this is where I'm going to stay till the God damned war's over. I'm for the 'sweet-life' from now on."

"Can't say that I blame you, Fred. It goes on and on, and doesn't seem to do anybody any good. Least of all, the poor peasants in the rice-paddies and you young fellows learning the art of war, instead of the disciplines of peace."

"It's not just a matter of stopping the Commies either, and in any case, you can't stop those bastards with bullets. Only by beating them at their own game. And that means the West has to offer a better way of living: with more justice and social-advancement than their system provides. In my experience, we aren't doing this and that's why I've personally opted out of the war-game. It is counter-productive: what with many of our best youngsters dying out there and those that survive becoming drug-addicts and perverts. Not that I'm against drugs in moderation but some of the guys are stoned most of the time: nothing to do except wait and listen and watch until the action starts."

"Yes it was tough for you out there. Anyway, forget it now Fred; come on over for supper with us tonight. Jean is doing an Arabic stewed-meat and veg with couscous."

"OK that sounds great! Tell her I'll be over about seven. Can we start work on the car tomorrow morning?"

"Yes; we'll strip her down: then I may have to get new parts from Agadir!"

Evening crept up on all the motley collection of tourists, tramps, draft-dodgers, scroungers and bohemian hippy types: and a few shaggy-looking surfers, strolling by Fred's tent, on to their own variously assorted abodes, proudly embracing their colourful surf-boards as though they represented some new form of masculine totem-pole around which must be displayed (to the chagrin of non-surfers) a bovine tribal orthodoxy of group-behaviour.

Those who did not show any obvious sign of belonging to any well-defined group were ignored: such as the gentle old ladies and gentlemen, with shrunk shanks, fat bellies and grey hair: who wandered along at this hour, exercising themselves and their pedigree dogs: whilst hoping, without success, that the sand and stones would not get between their toes and blister their feet. These stalwart individuals, in character, if frail in body; did at least choose their company freely and clung to no special cypher or symbols, which might narrow the true feelings of fellowship down to group-conformity. These people (let me repeat) were usually eyed with suspicion and treated with indifference by the young 'emancipated freethinkers', 'free-lovers' and convinced kif-smokers and surf-riders. The few youngsters who did relate to older, maturer people were the exception rather than the rule. Thus, instead of a healthy community-spirit developing, along the excitingly barbaric-ridge of coastline, just above the sandy beach which was, twice-daily washed clean by the industrious Atlantic rollers, there developed, or rather happened, a hotchpotch of tightly-knit groups which festered inwardly, rather than developed, by showing curiosity, interest and tolerance outwardly, towards each other.

Fred, was an exception in this respect, for he had struck up a friendship with the British aeroplane pilot and his family, who came from the island of Mull and a genuine, if somewhat tentative, relationship with Nigel Roberts, from Broughton, near Chester: a rather testy, crotchety old bachelor-teacher, who believed that the world was hurtling towards disaster and who spent most of his time making wind-wheel generators, which never seemed to work, unless it was blowing a hurricane. Fred liked the guy, just enough to sit round the camp fire, together with Andy and his family. On odd nights, when he felt in the mood, Nigel made a great bowl of soup and invited six or seven regular campers over for supper. The guests had to bring their own bottle though, as everyone was on a tight budget: because they wanted to stay and enjoy the mysterious beauty of the Moroccan scene and the strange fascination that Muslim-culture provides, as an additional back-drop to the immediate pleasures and enjoyments of camping on this untamed beach.

Beneath the mixture of life-styles: the flamboyant, hedonistic, dignified and the opportunist; lay the complexities of motivation: self-fulfilment: and the vague searchings and longings for some new hope; fresh vision and deep convictions that had, until now, evaded most of them.

The one solid fact appreciated by some but unconsciously rejected by many; was, that they were all existing at the same time in roughly the same place. "When two or three are gathered together in my name, there also I shall be."

2

What a sad reflection it was, for Nigel to note, that so many opportunities to meet in mind, body and spirit, were neglected and instead of trying to promote and cultivate each others' good: most preferred to remain much the same as when they arrived: except for the patient strokes of gold brown that the sun painted upon the bodies of all assembled there.

Fred's early boyhood spent in and around Greenwich Village, New York, with his deserted mother and all the tough, even squalid things he'd had to do to survive in and out of 'high-school': such as selling speed-pills inside and having his friend burst in and take polaroid shots of him sleeping with homosexual men outside, so that he could blackmail them, in order to help his mother pay the rent: then call-up and all the training and psychological-conditioning which brain-washed a guy, until he could only think of killing Commies and defending the constitution of the good old mother-fucking USA. Followed in the fullness-of-time with two years active-service in South Vietnam:

mostly on combat-duty.

All this hadn't helped Fred to grow up into what one might call a self-respecting, God-fearing boy. But his Vietnam experiences had dipped his soul, rather brutally, into the fires of life and he had come out of it coarsely tempered but by no means eroded! He still had a lot of fire in his belly and took rather a large all-round view of life: not getting too upset at the surprises and whimsical reverses that the laws of chance, coupled with yearnings for wider freedom sought in an alien culture, can provide.

Anyway there was a good supper in the offing; the ramshackle old car would be in service tomorrow with a bit of luck; and Amanda had offered to sleep with him this very night, so long as he agreed to come on over and sleep in her tent.

Fred locked the big Arabic, mahogany Pilgrim-box, which the crafty old dealer in the souk at Fez, had said was as old as time itself, and had accompanied dozens of the devout and the faithful Muslim-pilgrims to Mecca and back, and that the metal bindings, on all corners and three times round the trunk, were of solid-bronze: made by hand and the lock designed by a 'Fez' craftsman. His Goulimime-beads, worth three hundred dollars, were carefully hidden in the false bottom of the trunk and his few remaining traveller's cheques were in the leather bag, under his new kaftan. So, all was secure and he took a swim before supper: just to sharpen his healthy appetite.

Amanda had the same idea and didn't she look just like a Greek goddess there, sat on the rock! They both plunged in: recklessly wrestling with each other and the strong rolling waves, as they roared over the flat sea-sculptured beach. With the water dripping off them, like dancing diamonds sparkling in the rays of the dying sun, they both chased each other, laughingly, along until they dried off and were exhausted.

"See you tonight then, about ten-thirty. I've had an invite to supper with the Blacks from Scotland: So, 'fare ye well, my pretty maid'."

Amanda Shields from Lancing, England liked the big handsome boy from New York, who made such a joke out of life. He exhibited such bovine gusto: not caring so much about consequences but caring more for the action and the drama involved in personal encounters. She replied laughingly. "OK, don't make a pig of yourself: I don't want to sleep with a boar."

3

"Have some more Fred, there's plenty left," Jean served seconds to the men and Linda said she was full up and hadn't any room left for the banana-trifle that Jean had thoughtfully prepared and covered with her last tin of double whipped cream. She enjoyed Fred's company, more than she would like to admit, and wanted to give him a good impression of British home-cooking. "When I bought the meat down at the village this morning, I had my doubts about Arab-cleanliness with all the flies around; so I asked him to get me a piece out of the fridge. He charged me a little more: but I think it's worth it."

"Yes Jean, it's delicious. I suppose goat-meat has very little fat on it. Rather like venison but a little lighter in colour."

"One has to cook it like the Arabs though: slowly in an earthen-ware casserole-dish in the oven, or in a modern stainless-steel one, on a very low gas, together with plenty of red-peppers garlic and vegetables. Then the couscous is cooked, merely by adding the boiling stock from the casserole-dish."

"Yes, the old Arabs know a thing or two when it comes to food and cooking," chipped in Andy. "I've never seen such an abundance of fresh veg and fruit, at such ridiculously low prices. The three of us live well here, on about sixty-dirhams per week." (About five pounds.)

Conversation wound itself round culinary, domestic and financial matters. When it flagged, Andy proffered more red wine and then, after coffee, he put a bottle of Teacher's whisky on the small folding-table of the mobile home.

The Moroccan night outside had not intruded until a feint tap at the door heralded the presence, when Jean looked out, of a slightly built, thin-faced Arab boy, clad in a tightly fitting scull-cap and a dirty grey-coloured djellaba who propped up his ancient bicycle with one thin leg and sinuously extricated a couple of doughnuts from the rear-end box, "Salaam! Salaam! Very nice fresh cakes, for sweet English lady: special price. One fifty for two; four for two-fifty."

"Shall I get a couple Andrew?"

"Please yourself my love. You're the boss in these matters. How about you Fred? Do you feel like risking a dose of Arab-tummy tomorrow?"

"Not for me, Andy. I've had a fine meal which couldn't possibly be improved upon."

"Oh, but he looks so thin and tired and he's so young to be out working at this hour." She fished in her purse and paid the boy for two and off he sped with a grateful smile on his boyish face.

"He's probably a spy ready to tip off some old rascal in the village which tents and vans are unguarded or easy to rob."

44

"You've got such a suspicious nature! Thinking bad of an innocent little boy like him!"

"Finish off you're drink Fred, and we can take a walk along the beach. Just for a constitutional and to see if everything is OK, whilst Jean puts Linda to bed and washes the dishes."

"Sorry Andy, I'll have to be going now! I'm meeting Amanda in about five minutes."

"OK, see you tomorrow, you lucky devil. Have a nice time!"

Fred stepped outside and saw the familiar fire burning in the hole near to Nigel's car, and a couple of shadowy figures crouched over it eating a late supper cooked on an Arabic tagine stove. They exchanged anaemic 'Good-nights' with each other and Fred strode over to an awaiting Amanda, who had spent the last half-hour at the camp-fire and was now lighting a small candle inside her tent. The dimly-lit Arab village ran away over to the left, made a little more visible than usual by the half-moon that shone from a clear untroubled sky.

Fresh-faced, intelligent, twenty-two-year-old Amanda, was feeling just a little uneasy about her life here, in this savage country, where nothing was predictable or regular. Even the surfers, whom she liked quite a lot, behaved differently, as though some of the wild beauty and unknown culture of the place had got into their blood. Most of them smoked kif and slept around with girls whenever they got the chance and it all seemed to be done at such a low-key. One girl, apparently, was as good as another, and yet she had hoped for security, a worth-while relationship, that would lead to a 'we' situation instead of just, amorphous-sex, ending in petulant and sometimes undignified, 'see you around's', or an indifferent 'Thanks a lot, Amanda. Chow,

chow's'. etc. Perhaps Fred would have more style. He certainly had more personality than the rest, anyway: so that was something to go on. Oh, how she missed her Sony tape-recorder and her nice clean bedroom back home. The conversation with Nigel and Tom, one of the older surfers, who liked to go in with the youngsters, just to show that the 'oldies' weren't so decrepit, had upset her quite a bit and what with the roar of the waves surging over the darkened flats and the moon twinkling down from a foreign sky she needed the reassurance of a loving man: someone who would take her in his arms and give.

Nigel had spoken of 'Affluence destroying God in the West', and as she listened to them both, whilst she drank her bowl of soup, she dug down deep into her own life, to see if what they said could be vindicated by her own knowledge of affairs, and the sudden gush of frighteningly new experiences that had thrust themselves upon her since leaving home for this 'Moroccan holiday'.

"Yes Tom. I'm afraid we've had it in the West. The so-called Third-world is emerging, and thrusting between the Super-powers with remarkable skill. One of my teacher colleagues in Saudi-Arabia, remained after his term of service and became a Muslim and he is very happy to have escaped from the trivial materialist society of the West."

"As you know, Nigel, I taught for a while in an Arabic school in Cairo and one day Abdul Jahwad, a student friend from my college-days, walked into the Madrassa school, Al Thaager. He was a gymnastics-inspector so we resumed our former friendship in Cairo. He then had modern ideas: drank a little and enjoyed pop-music; played around with girls and wore European clothes.

"In sixty-nine he took his pilgrimage to Mecca, as all good Muslims must do at least once in their lives. He stayed there for one month; the Holy month of 'Al Hajj'. And when he returned I arranged to fix a little party of a few friends to welcome his home-coming. He arrived rather late and apologetic, but quite determined never, ever, to drink alcohol, or to eat pork, or to listen to Western trashy-music, or even to play around any more. I have never seen such a change take place in any man, as with Abdul Jahwad."

"Well, that fits my own experience of trying, without success, to adjust once more to the culture that spawned me. But I find it quite impossible, after being with Muslim colleagues and seeing how human, friendly and tolerant they are, compared with the elitist-groups and coteries and professional-cliques, in the technical-West. There, in Saudi-Arabia, at least they simplify their problems: we unnecessarily complicate them and manufacture neurosis and complexes just as certainly as we mass-produce those trivial goods and services that we so avidly consume. So that now-a-days no one who is affluent can take a holiday, unless he or she is loaded down with electric tooth-brushes, shavers, hair-dryers, food-mixers, refrigerators and washing-machines. Of course the young come away with next to nothing. For we live selfishly without any inspiration coming from each other, or from God. Thus, a good Muslim endures his poverty with more dignity than a rich Westerner enjoys the ownership of his high-powered Jaguar and his expensive yacht moored at Cowes, on the Isle of White. It's a matter of priorities: The ancient cultures of India and China are modernising slowly but surely, without turning their citizens into automated spiritually-castrated eunuchs."

This was strong stuff for a young girl on her own, in a foreign environment. It made her very moody, thoughtful and a little less sure of her own values.

Now he was cosily beside her, stretched out luxuriously, with a pulsating aura of abandonment to the things of the moment and responding to her own mood as best he could.

4

The candle was beginning to flare, because the wick was too long: so she rose gracefully from a lying position and trimmed it whilst Fred took the opportunity to put his arms right round her breasts; held her firm and kissed her passionately on the back of her neck and under her left-ear. She popped her nail-scissors back into her bag: stuffed it under her pillow and lent over and embraced him with a deep sigh of relief and said, "Oh Fred, hold me tight and don't let me go." This he did and she searched his face, in the flickering light, for recognition; true acceptance and honourable-love. She thought that she saw it for a brief moment. But Fred's such a carefree, joker-of-a-man. Could he really mean anything that he said or did?

She unloaded her heart to him about the short conversation she'd just listened to at the fire. "Don't take those two old codgers too seriously Amanda: They're past it you know, an' all 'oldies' can do is look back on their own miss-spent youth and blame the youth of today for doing what they themselves did when they were young! Only they did it with more secretiveness than we do. Don't you think that we are, at least, more emotionally honest than they were? More open and natural with each other?"

"Yes, but what do we mean by those two words? Can't 'open' mean unselective and wanton, and can 'natural', abandoned and unscrupulous?"

Fred had enjoyed a superb day: ending it with an

excellent free meal and he didn't want the day to be spoilt with an academic discussion of sex mores, or tortuous assessments of life-styles and their accompanying sets of value-judgements. All he knew, at present, was that he felt as randy as hell and he was in the company of one of the most bed-worthy chicks he'd ever slept with in his life.

Amanda lay back onto the double-sized sleeping-bag snuggled up to Fred and felt warmth and comfort coming from his strong body. All her confusions fled. She was soon intoxicated with pleasurable sensations as Fred explored her beautiful body with gentle, yet strong manly fingers. She'd taken a pill about six hours ago, so everything would be OK even if they got very involved!

Fred's movements became more exciting as she responded to his ardent caresses. He threw off his light Arabic kaftan and lay back for a while temporarily exhausted with his explorations. They were both naked now and Amanda blew out the candle.

The shape of him was even more stimulating in the half-light that peeped into the small tent from the moon-lit sky and she bent over him and kissed his sex, gently taking him into her sensitive mouth. Fred was out of his mind with sensuous delight. She ran her delicate fingers lightly up and down on the inside of both legs at once, until his stomach hardened and his breath came in deep gulps, expiring each breath from his straining body with deep sighs of inner peace.

She stopped, lay back and looked at him proudly, with deep affection in her hazel eyes. "You're wonderful, Fred: so different! Sometimes you're so passive."

Fred said nothing: but in turn, lent over and kissed her whole body from head to toe until, just at the right moment, he entered her . . . so gently and tenderly. She nearly

49

c

swooned in ecstacy.

"Oh Fred, it's never happened like this before. I've never felt so confident, so sure, as I feel with you!" His movements began slowly, with a beautiful rhythm that ended in a crescendo of sexual joy for both, as they lay back, locked in an embrace that only 'Eros' can evoke.

They slept until six in the morning and both felt so refreshed they took a swim whilst naked, in the calm ebb-tide and returned once more to their loving.

At nine, it was broad daylight and both felt hungry so Amanda made tea and boiled four eggs for breakfast, whilst Fred went over to his tent for some bread and a pot of marmalade. He was sold on English-breakfasts these days and didn't feel he'd eaten unless he finished off with toast and jam.

5

His tent sagged at the back, as two guy-lines seemed to have loosened during the night. Perhaps a camper had stumbled over them on returning from the village last night, Fred thought light-heartedly to himself as he entered, after pulling up the zipper at the front. Light entered the tent through a large slit, just above where he had safely locked up his box the previous night. "Suffering sons of Eros," he said, appropriately enough. "What in the name of all Christendom and Islam has happened here?" His eyes told him plainly enough his box had gone. Yanked unceremoniously through the slit in the canvas. His Vietnam-self returned tempestuously. He was ready to fight: to tear and rip someone to pieces. He dashed outside, followed the trail of widely-scuffed markings in the sand, then the bent grass and rough foliage, down into a hollow about one hundred metres from his ridge-tent. There it lay upturned: lid broken open and all his gear strewn around. He soon found his empty Moroccan leather purse, collected his belongings together into a pile and inspected the inside of the trunk. "Oh, thank Christ! The bastards haven't stolen my Goulimime beads."

Andy had seen him running over the ground like a blood-hound having found the scent and came walking over with Linda. "Can we help you Fred?"

"Yes please, Andy. I've been ripped off! All my traveller's cheques and loose money. Thank God I had my passport with me in my kaftan pocket. I found the car documents too, so that's OK."

"What's the damage, Fred?"

"Oh, about sixty dollars all together."

"Quite a loss to bear though; and you no job and not much saved up over in the States!"

"Yes, quite a rip-off, but I've still got about three hundred dollars in Goulimime-beads and when Jean sews them up into arm-bracelets they'll be worth six-dollars each back home."

"Yes, the wife was telling me that she's going to get working on them for you. But how are you going to live right now, with no loose money?"

"Well, there's only one thing that I can think of at the moment and that is to get the car fixed today, go down to Tan Tan in the South and try and do a deal of some sort. As you know the beads act as currency down there, so perhaps I can sell a load of them for a fair price and become solvent again."

"Come on then. Let's start on the motor. I feel just in the mood for getting stuck in to some real work! How's

Amanda taken it?"

"Not told her yet! I'm just going over to finish breakfast, then I'll join you for the repair-job."

"OK, see you in about ten minutes."

"You'd better stay here Amanda, I'll only be away about one or two days and so if you don't mind I'll put my gear in your tent for safety."

"Sure Fred: you just do what you think is best. Remember I'll be here waiting for you my love." She said this self-consciously: even guiltily, for inescapably both were involved in the human guilt that produces cosmic changes in the quality of life for all. For aren't we all 'a part of each other' as the Buddhists believe. If only she had gone over to his tent, instead of inviting him to her's. Then he'd have never been robbed. Had she been wrong in the first place to desire him. Do not our eyes beget desire and are therefore traitors to our very souls! Stimulating desire, when our thoughts are away from God. Did she do it, just as a sexual-experiment, to find out if Fred was a better performer in bed than the surfers: two of whom she had slept with?

What was the reality of her being? Last night was so real, such a comfort, even a revelation in terms of sexual loving, but didn't true love include everything, compassion redemption and even sacrifice of one's self for one's beloved?

Overnight she had become an important part of the drama of Fred's life as well as her own. She had tried to give him so much: but was it just an 'ego-trip': a kind of ritualised mutual-masturbation exercise: even with her fine sentiments and generous womanly-giving to this American army-deserter from New York.

Seen in the cold light of reason, it didn't add up. How could she be loyal to him? A man without a home; who had burnt his boats and was 'persona-none-grata' in his own country. A man who had forsaken everything that American Democracy stands for and who was now, after the robbery, closer to penury than he was before. And then what? When his meagre funds dried-up: or if he failed to sell his beads down in Tan Tan, she'd have to support him out of her small budget, and then what? She continued to ask herself with remorseless logic. Go back to England together: helping him to settle and find work in a strange country, whilst living as man and wife? What would her friends think, her, of all people, marrying a deserter?

6

Perhaps the Arab culture was correct, keeping women secretly tucked away: protected from men, temptations and their own vulnerability. Wasn't 'love' over romanticised in the West and even trivialised? Didn't true love grow slowly; like a delicate plant being carefully nurtured? Wasn't the whole idea of romantic-love just an illusion: generated by exhibitionism and supported with permissiveness.

She put on her clean bikini-set and walked over to where the two men were already taking off the cylinder-head, which revealed a faulty-gasket a broken stud at the front of the head. "Well, what's the verdict this time? Think you can fix it?" She asked in a neutral voice.

Andy looked at her lustrous hair and beautiful sensuous-body and replied non-committally. "Hope so my sweet, for lover-boy's sake."

Fred grinned knowingly at Andy's cheerful wink.

"I'll have to file my teeth up and start chewing at that broken stud unless your lover-boy can bite as well as he can kiss; then I'll leave that job to him."

"Just pass me those dog-grips Andy, and I'll have this brute out in a jiffy."

Fred eased it out, whilst Andy decoked the head and then he said, "Come on the two of you: let's go into town and buy a new stud, gasket and points and with a bit of luck, she'll be fixed by four o'clock."

"Sure you don't mind, Andy? You know that I can't pay you except with Goulimime beads?"

"They'll do," said the practical Scot. "It's almost worth doing the job for nothing for King Fred, the biggest male sex-symbol for miles around! And in any case it's heaven to be away from the wife just now. She's got 'em in at the moment and she's always difficult to manage for three or four days every month. As you know Fred, women always go through a period of psychological disintegration once a month and I think the old Arabs have got their heads screwed on the right way by keeping 'em locked up when they are like that and not letting 'em have much freedom, even when they're normal, which is very seldom if I know women."

Amanda walked slowly away from the two men after saying that she would stay behind and guard the tents. As she went, she gave Andy a strange penetrating look of rebellious candour, as much as to say: "You male chauvinist pigs!" Bloody male philistines: Men and women are always poles apart, she thought moodily as she splashed into the water, not knowing whether she wanted to swim or just to get away from these utterly inscrutable, unknowable males.

At four o'clock, after a tough trek round Agadir for parts and a late sandwich-lunch of cold ham, salad and beer, the job was finished and there she was ticking-over, as good as gold. King Fred took Andy for a short trip along the coastal-road and they both returned with exultant looks of triumph on their sunburnt faces. Fred drove masterfully and Andy declared the car good for at least twenty-five-thousand kilometres if the battery didn't drop through the corroded front-boot and if the tyres were renewed all-round and if Fred didn't drive flat out all the time!

7

"Come on boys, jump in. I'll take you to the village."

A group of surfers squashed gratefully into the small car, clad in shorts only, and instead of walking the couple of kilometres they arrived at the village shops with King Fred ponderously settled into the small driving-seat and the car parked near a crowd of Arab boys and men who were idling the heavy, sun-soaked afternoon away in the cool shade of the trees and the awnings above the few shops just off the main highway. They tumbled out of the car in a disorderly array of bare-torsos, sunburnt thighs and shaggy-hair and the djellaba-clad Arabs, especially the young boys, looked on eagerly at this live, television-show in colour. "What impudence these foreigners possessed."

They entered the dark, cool, tall-walled interior of the green-grocer's first. "What'll we get, Jake?" In just as feckless a fashion as they enter their Woolworth's store (but clad more appropriately) back in their home towns in the UK.

"Oh, veg; fruit; bread. Oh, an' some sugar an' milk an' some eggs."

They all trooped into the shop exhibiting bulging muscles and tight, well filled bathing-shorts and the Arabs nearby took more than a passing interest in the best-formed boy of the group.

"Ah, take no notice of this stupid load of old queers. They'll have your arse if you don't watch out," said Robert to Peter who had a fine body.

"I wouldn't dare walk around here at night on my tod!" replied Pete. "They'd grab your arse and screw you on the spot: the randy load of old goats."

"Yes they're sex-starved, that's what it is. They eat too much shish kebab," said Jake, who looked as though he himself was a good deal too well-fed.

"Well, come on, pay the gentleman and stop pissing about with those trinkets if you're not buying them," remonstrated Robert.

Peter, who had picked up a bracelet with a colourful Goulimime-bead threaded onto a strongly woven leather thong said, "Fred's got some of these stones! They're beautiful!"

Outside Fred was having a little trouble with the aspiring motor-mechanic of the neighbourhood. One young fellow was trying to lift the front boot and another was hanging on the back of the saloon, hoping for a ride when the car rolled. So Fred eased his great bulk out of the seat, and this movement was enough to send them scattering away, up the dingy street in gleeful delight at having got a typical reaction from the exercise of their curiosity, even if it fell short of satisfying their deep desire to know more about mechanical things, especially car engines.

At least one thing was sure, thought Fred, as he drove the four back to camp, King Fred would have another free meal tonight, in return for this free taxi ride. So he felt that things weren't working out too badly after all!

They lost a hubcap, off the front left-wheel, somewhere along the dust-track whilst returning: for Fred showed off a little, bumping the car up, rather violently, from the main-road. Fred swirled to a halt in a cloud of dusty sand, well pleased with himself and his little bus.

The boys never found the dust-cap, so Andy said, "Not to worry. A yogurt plastic cup will just about fit." And it did: so that was that.

Fred took supper with the boys, who invited Amanda over also: after Fred had dropped the hint that he'd like them to 'look after her' whilst he was away, down in Tan Tan. Amanda was a little embarrassed, for she knew all about Peter and Jake and didn't really want to know any more: but she was diplomatic and laughingly agreed to lend Fred forty dirhams for petrol, to make sure, at least, that he got there and back.

He bade farewell to her and his new found 'Limey' friends. ("You've got to show these Limey cock-suckers just how cool a real Yankee is, in matters of driving and fucking and doing big-deals down in Tan Tan.") And his headlights could be seen stabbing the darkening sky above the highway as his car jerked up on to it; and he swung away in the direction of that last out-post of civilisation in southern Morocco, before the desert takes over and only camels, high-wheeled trucks and Rovers, driven carefully, can make the trip to El Aaiún, in Spanish Sahara (now divided between Morocco and Mauritania). All his friends had wished him well and hoped that the trip would be a profitable one.

He sat back, put his foot down and roared confidently along the moonlit road, enjoying the cool-breeze feeding in through the quarter-window. These European cars were so small and cramped a guy up, but he found the seat-lever and yes, it still worked: so he eased his long legs more comfortably into the well.

8

At Sidi Ifni, he stopped and was just going into a small café when a young couple came up and asked if he was going to Tan Tan? "Yes, that's my direction. Can I give you a lift?" he said in anticipation of their eager looks at the vehicle.

"Oh, yes please! We've been stuck here for five hours and hoped to make it to Tan Tan tonight."

"Well, look, I've been robbed back in Tarhjicht so I'll have to ask you to share petrol costs: that is, unless you would like to buy some Goulimime beads?"

"Let's have a coffee in the bar here and maybe we'll look at what you've got," said the Canadian boy. "We did intend to stop off at Goulimime, but the guy who drove us down to here was in a hurry and didn't stop off there."

"Well, what do you think of them?" asked Fred, as he poured about half a kilo onto the small table. "These are the very best ones and worth six dollars a'piece in the States. You can have them for five each.

He didn't tell them that they were still north-west of Goulimime and that he'd taken the coast-road to evade the police patrols as he hadn't a current driving-licence or insurance at the moment, because of the time-factor and his impecunious state, and he didn't say that he had purchased the beads from an Arab merchant for fifty dollars the lot (three kilos) on his upward journey: crossing over from Las Palmas to Spanish Sahara and hitching a lift to that interesting camel-trading centre; where the town-square is so full of buildings that are decorated with Arabesque-arches, which he had found so sexually stimulating because they reminded him of the male-organ with a circumsised crown. He had looked his present clients over and decided that they were the kind of youngsters who hadn't been in Morocco long and they washed their clothes often and rinsed them out five times before hanging them up to dry. So he was safe taking them for a ride. They looked affluent enough to pay five for each anyway.

"Well, you don't give us much choice, do you?" the handsome boy said. "We'll settle for five each, at that price, if you think that will help?"

"Right, done," said Fred. They carefully chose the best of the bunch that Fred had on display: getting quite ecstatic about the wonderful colours. But the girl was not too pleased with the shape of them. (About an inch and a half long, three-quarters thick: round-shaped with a small hole through the middle.)

They paid over fifty Canadian dollars and Fred said, "OK, the drinks are on me, plus a free ride to Tan Tan."

They passed through Goulimime soon after and Fred said he didn't know this small town. Anyway, it was pretty well blacked-out and he avoided the centre and was soon onto the narrow strip-road, leading to the south.

They arrived at half past mid-night and Fred said, "Bye bye, I hope you have fun in Las Palmas."

He looked around, booked in at the Al Haramain Hotel and slept the sleep of all lone-individuals who have taken on the world as they find it.

The 'life-force' was strong in him the next day and he felt in a mood for jubilant celebration, so he toured the sleazy cafés and the market-area which he knew quite well.

"Come back this evening at seven and I'll have the kif ready for you." The old rascally looking antique dealer had said, when he sauntered into the old shop with everything in it, from modern cassette tape-recorders, to old brass and bronze teapots, trays, tagine-stoves and hand-woven Persian-carpets. "Two Kilos for one Kilo of beads, OK?"

"Eawah (Yes)," he said, as though swearing an oath of loyalty to the words of the Holy Koran.

Fred saw a beautiful Arab-girl without a veil go into The Al Jedida Café, so tripped in dutifully after her and sat down at her table. There weren't many people about at this hour, so she was pleased to speak with this big, healthy, sensuous-looking American. Besides, she was nearly broke too, so perhaps he would be generous and pay for her drink.

Jamilla had seen this big bluff, easy-going American in the souk (market) earlier that morning and was flattered that he had followed her into this café. Just before he entered, she was in a nostalgic reverie about her most recent boyfriend. 'Manolo', she called him (the familiar form). His full name being Manuel Garcia, cabaret-dancer in the Cintra night-club in Las Palmas.

She left Manolo after a tempestuous row due to his jealous rage, because she had accepted a dry vermouth from a soft-spoken blond-haired boy from New England, America. She left in a huff, last Friday night.

Jamilla knew that she was attractive enough to call the tune with most men who were fascinated with her impeccable Arabic beauty and so she'd stomped out and with her last money she had crossed over to El Aalún by boat. How dynamic the capitalist West really was and how exciting for an emancipated daughter of a rich Lebanese-merchant of Christian background.

They had a sincere talk about travel and he filled her in discreetly about his war experiences and the traumas; facing death; disease and loneliness in the forests of Vietnam and his later difficult decision to give it all up and flee from the USA, and subsequently, his efforts to build a new life-style for himself here in Morocco.

She, for her turn, explained her own form of alienation and her search for new freedoms away from home and the cosmopolitan sophistications of life as lived in the city of Bayreuth. Her mother had died in a road-accident and her father married again and she couldn't get on with her step-mother, and so after her education and finishing as a private paying-scholar at the American university there, she had left home: prepared to make her own way in life. She'd had various receptionist posts and had done a little dancing and professional striptease work in Istanbul, Paris and London: finally ending up at 'Manolo's' nightclub, in Las Palmas.

They had lunch together and she decided that she liked him and would book in at the Al Haramain Hotel and keep him company, so they went back and he cancelled his single and booked a double and they walked about round the town until it was time for Fred to pick his 'stuff' up.

After they had douched together. Jamilla seeing Fred in the flesh: how bronzed and long legged he was: and he'd seen how she curved voluptuously everywhere, the white tiled bath-room emphasising the delicious chocolate coloured skin that made her into a perfect work of art. The straight jet-black hair unloosed from the bronze hair clip: the thick sensuous lips and her face showing high cheek-bones, a dominant Arabic-nose, set between large black eyes that sparkled from below a serene brow. They both changed thoughtfully: Fred into a grey djellaba and Jamilla into a blue kaftan-style dress with gold piping down the hems.

How different she was from an English girl, much more subtle and sinuous, especially in the lower regions. He was going to enjoy loving Jamilla. He could hardly wait but business before pleasure. He must be in a financial position to treat her as befits her looks.

He was very impressed with her! She'd just helped him on with his Arab gown and combed his hair out! Then she took up her polished leather Moroccan handbag and they both strode along arm-in-arm to the antique dealer's shop.

She stood demurely outside, looking at the gowns in the shop next door, wondering what sort of a deal Fred was making? So closed and uncommunicative these Westerners! Well, she'd get to know all about him in due course. Most men could be read as easily as a book. It was only a matter of time.

He came out looking well pleased with a brown paper-parcel which he tucked away in his capacious pocket. He took her eagerly by the arm and they meandered down the high-street and found a good-class restaurant.

She sipped her vermouth and said, "You should have been born an Arab. You like it over here don't you?"

"Yes love, I like it well enough. It's so different to the States. There's not much social frame-work over there. Everyone is a go-getter, out for themselves in a free-for-all scramble. The strongest or the most unscrupulous come out on top: the rest go to the wall. Here, every man and woman has his place and although there is a rich variety of life within the framework, the outlines of economic and social life are clearly drawn for everyone to understand."

"Yes, there's not much choice outside the social-proprieties, especially for women. Men are much freer to come and go with each other. But there's no 'permissiveness' between boys and girls the same as in the Christian-quarter of Bayreuth or the West generally. In the Lebanon, these customs are breaking down, but not here in the south of Morocco."

"In the West, life is getting to be just one big 'ego-trip' with materialism and personal possessions being the main life-goals. From this you get power-politics involving spheres of influence and the god-damned wars, to protect business interests and national influence and prestige. I'm just hoping to negotiate a big loan from an American Bank of say around twenty-thousand dollars: go to Shanghai, buy a big Chinese Junk, sail it back to the States, say California or Miami, and sell it for thirty-five-thousand to one of them rich millionaires over there. Then with the profit try and buy a piece of land over here in Morocco and forget all about the good old USA."

He drank up his Schweppes tonic with ice. They enjoyed a chicken with mushroom sauce dinner and after fresh fruit and coffee they returned, happily a'tuned.

Fred had to forget the uncertainties and to some extent the responsibilities of his easy-going compromises with a wicked world, so he went to the bathroom; rolled a couple of joints, just to try the quality of the 'stuff' before returning to Tarhjicht, in order to sell some to the campers along the coast there. He climbed into bed alongside Jamilla and offered her one.

"Yes I'll try just one," she said, "but normally I don't touch the 'stuff' because I've seen how dopey and sick the old Arabs are in the Arab quarter of Bayreuth through smoking it too much."

"Yes, I'm the same, I don't take much of it. You've got to keep your wits about you in this world if you are going to survive in it." They lay back smoking luxuriously. Soon they were lost in a dreamland of perfection, purity and sensuous love.

What wonderful lovers American males were, Jamilla thought passionately to herself, as he explored her, languorously at first then more ardently until he could contain himself no longer and opened her so gently. How much more sensitive white men were, at least those who had a normal foreskin. So much more delicate than the bare-crowned Arabs, who usually wasted little time in love-play prior to actual fucking. They were such purists but very strong and satisfying.

Two more days of sensual delight passed all too quickly for Fred, who began to have qualms of conscience about Amanda. So, after three nights and four days together, they paid up, packed their bags into the Seat and set off at three-thirty on Saturday afternoon.

9

Amanda settled into a desultory routine of reading, eating, occasional dips and lonely sleeping for the three nights following Fred's departure, only eased from this recipe of tedium by her nightly visits to Nigel's campfire, where the masculine talk and nourishing pots of soup somehow held her together.

Nigel and Tom were so orderly and regular in their habits. A hole was dug nearby for the refuse, another contained the tagine-stove, giving warmth and illumination on chilly nights to the visitors who sat on pieces of cardboard as these were warm, simple and inexpensive. A hand-made table supported the assortment of cups, glasses and bottles of wine and so the fire became a focal point and the lighting, something of a ritual for the two 'oldies' who found drift-wood a cheap source of fuel, paid for by an enjoyable walk along the beach to collect it. Andy and Jean sat inside their van at night except when they were nervous and got on each other's nerves, then they would come out to the fire. Andy taking over as raconteur and amusing all present with his ribald accounts of old ladies getting tipsy, swooning with fear and even pissing themselves when the planes he piloted hit bumpy-weather, or came in for a difficult landing.

Tonight, being Saturday, the third of February nineteen-seventy-two, efforts at conversation and the consequent growth in community-spirit had petered out. Nigel had been robbed, mysteriously, three weeks earlier, which accounted for his spartan way of life at present and now, only five days ago, Fred's life had fundamentally changed, for he too had been ripped off. The consumer-society which they had all tried to escape from, for a time, was rearing its ugly head. They would all have to be returning to business, etcetera, soon, and what had this holiday meant to each of them?

The German Bundesbank-secretary, Frieda Dietritch and her fiancé, Hermann Schartz, who was a computer-programmer sat close: listening; drinking wine and wondering about the world of Islam out there in Agadir, Fez, Marrakesh and even the small, ill-lit banana-village nearby. All so frighteningly wild yet simple and dignified. So different to the hyper-technocracy that Germany is.

These people made nearly everything that they required by hand and despised machinery, as Germans despise wasting time and people who aren't rich.

Earnest, a Belgian maths teacher, was telling a lewd story in the hopes of enlivening the doleful spirits of the group. He spoke English. "Three Moroccans on holiday in London," he said, "stopped outside a wine and spirits shop. Abdulla went inside and bought a bottle of Johnny Walker for three pounds, Ahmed went in and got a bottle for two pounds. Then Ali went in and bought the same whisky for one pound. The three Arabs were mystified by British business methods, as there had been no bargaining. They entered together, to find out about this method of conducting business. The shopkeeper said, 'My boss is fucking my wife up above and so I'm fucking his business here, down-below.' "

The conversation had reached a new low even for this anaemic group of vastly superior technocrats! All the way along the escarpment small coteries and specialist groups like the surfers, were idling their time away, in escapist, drug-inspired reveries of make-believe, and the richer more elderly groups getting quietly drunk on cheap Moroccan wine.

10

The mythological idea that they were superior had to be supported, in the last analysis, by making comparisons and so Paul spoke next. Paul a gymnastics teacher from Bruxelles in Belgium said, "Well, I don't think much of their youths, so thin and under-weight, they never swim in the sea." Which wasn't quite true, because they did, further along the coast, when they had time off work: which wasn't very often.

"Neither do they parade around in shorts with various exhibitionist-captions sewn to them either," responded Nigel, with a little heat. "Like, 'I'm for sex-tension' or 'Dynamic movement' or 'Try before you buy', etc."

"Well, it's obvious isn't it?" went on Paul, "it's been on tele! These people aren't modern! They've never won the cup and they aren't democratic. They are governed by a feudal King and a load of old Muslim Holy Men and mufties who don't know their arse from their elbow. They are thousands of years behind the times."

How feeble their penetration into Muslim culture. How

slight their study of the anthropology of a people who live in a very hot country and who put Allah first in all things. How superficial their judgement of the Arab system of protecting their young girls and women. What a reproach there was in the quiet dignity of the shopkeepers who daily accepted the invasion of their shops with equanimity and religious fortitude. An acceptance that would be impossible in so-called 'democratic England', if for example, a group of Arab boys clad in their national dress were to invade Woolworths back home, or a small grocer's store at the corner of the street in Blackpool, Brighton, or Clacton.

Nigel tried a fresh gambit. "I've heard that Isfahan, Turkish and Moroccan carpets (hand-made), are all the rage in the swish London stores these days. People are buying them as a hedge against inflation."

Frieda and Hermann both agreed and Frieda said, "We are thinking of doing the same. We are hoping to buy a couple before we return to Germany?"

"Why is it, do you think, that value attaches to hand-made goods from this country and machine-produced lose their value quickly?"

"Perhaps because they are prettier and made from genuine sheep's wool. I really don't know."

"Isn't it because we are starved of touching things and seeing things that were made for the joy of making them?" chipped in Tom. "And that the culture that allows its citizens to follow their heart's longings is in a subtle, almost indefinable way, superior or at least as good as our own."

Everyone fell quiet at this point in the comparative discussion reflecting upon what had been said, when a car's lights indicated a turn off the main road onto the track leading to their part of the beach.

"Oh, perhaps it's Fred at last," exclaimed Amanda, who

had been very silent and deep within herself whilst all the talk had flowed back and forward. And indeed, it was Fred.

"What is life if we never do those things that are closest to our heart's desire?" continued Nigel, but his remarks were ignored for King Fred stepped out with Jamilla, his latest beautiful pick-up from Tan Tan.

Everyone moved round the circle, squashing up a bit to accommodate the pair of lovers. Amanda fell back, lost in inexplicable despair, only managing a feeble glance in his direction on the other side of the fire.

Andy and Jean joined the group for they'd seen the car swing in. They sat a little apart and didn't know the antecedents of the night's conversation. Andy rested his arm on Fred's large shoulder and said, "How was it, did you manage a profitable deal OK?"

"Oh yes, everything went fine," Fred replied, looking Jamilla passionately in the eyes.

He took out a few joints already rolled up and offered them to anyone who would like to indulge. "Have some soup Fred, and I've got plenty for your girlfriend too. It'll do you more good than dope after a long car journey."

"Yes please, we'd love some, thanks a lot."

"Why do you knock dope, Nigel? Fred knows his dope all right. He's old enough to know what he's doing."

"I didn't intend to 'knock dope' as you colloquially put it. I merely stated what is after all a fact. Food, after a long trip, at least warms the stomach and makes one comfortable and hopefully affable enough to yarn a bit."

Nigel turned to Tom for support, feeling that Andy had turned traitor and because of some deep complex reason, probably of a sexual nature, he was now embracing Fred right round the shoulders. Tom said, "Oh, don't take Andy too seriously Nigel, he's had too much to drink."

Jamilla sat close to Fred hoping that he would get high enough not to notice that she hadn't changed her underclothes for two days. The Germans and the two Belgian teachers smoked away and were in a separate world already. The fire died down and the calm ocean kissed the beach good-night.

The party dwindled sadly after this disagreeable set-to. With the dying embers glowing when wafted by the gentle breeze from the sea, they all said a feint-hearted, "Good night," to each other and departed . . .

The deep silence of the Arab night enveloped all in mystery and for the Europeans living under an Arab sky, a sterile day of repletion gave way to a sterile night of sex without true loving. For here no joy, no grace, no vitality came in. All ached to communicate, but there was no communion, for nothing human grew upon the barren sands of commercial competition, except the fears of failure and the strong weeds of aggressiveness against all competition.

These, after all, were the main expressions of their defeated lives.

4

Last Exit from Saudi Arabia

A detour sign for non-Muslims on the Mecca road out of Jiddah meant take a left towards Medina, another holy city but not quite so exclusive to Westerners, about two hundred kilometres north. I settled to the barren scene on either side except for an igneous crop of black rock forming a shallow gorge. Brilliant black against shades of rusty red desert then back to hazy shimmering dullness. Then the odd herd of goats, a camel train in the far distance on my left heading no doubt for Medina market where dates, figs, salt, spices or modern cassettes and videos are exchanged, sold or haggled over. Above flapped a few hungry looking vultures masking the sun in the afternoon heat haze.

Perhaps, almost certainly, I would never see the city of Jiddah again. Never enjoy such friendships and respect as I had enjoyed whilst teaching English language at Al Fallah madrassa. I didn't realise that though in those far off days of nineteen-seventy. I took so much for granted, my car, my Western confidence and even myself. I was healthy and my bank-balance was too. My VW Berliner performed well for one hundred k's then it died on me. Gauge? Still half full.

What the hell now? I asked of a leaden sky. The sultry heat vapourised the juice before reaching the carb's enforcing a halt. I found a culvert under a ramp and snoozed away the time after supping a cooler from the ice-box. Only light shorts on but still uncomfortably hot with no flowing breeze from mobility.

It is June nineteen-seventy. My teaching contract finished in May. I'd sold furnishings and let my flat off to Colin, a young teacher from Scotland, who was to teach English to mature students in the Saudi air-force. My present home, the VW, was full of books, grub, sleeping-bag, photos, spare-clothes, a few souvenirs and on the luggage-rack, a brand new tape-recorder; the latest Japanese model. Quite large compared with today's cassettes, radios and videos, and long before micro-chips.

I rested patiently till six, when the sun dipped and cooler air from the Red Sea came on shore in slight breezy gusts at first then a steady flow. Turned the ignition and she started first click. In no time . . . so it seemed . . . I'd passed Medina on my right. Known to travellers along this narrow asphalted road by its many tall minerettes and lights from a biggish city by Saudi standards, and it sharply reminded me of what I had experienced of Arabia, its Muslim religion, and the pathos of leaving my beloved Hamed behind. A born thief, but a superb friend who came closer to me than any other human on this earth. Not only personally centred nostalgia but linked to deep respect for the birth-place of Mohammed the prophet in this city of Medina almost fourteen centuries ago.

So by slow degrees my whole personality, character or whatever equation I was, would have to adapt to what I knew to be a rather sterile spiritual desert, growing out of material abundance in Europe. The grace and dignity of human relationships in the Arab world are not the product of politics or religious education so much as the ability to live in a very difficult part of the world where sand, sun and Allah dictate their own terms of reference and woe betide if these three are not obeyed. Hence compassion, brotherly-love, and sympathies having a chance to grow. If these precious values were not an integral part of Arab culture, then travellers would die in the desert.

Yambio was my next main stopping point but I guessed I'd find a small wayside oasis with café and petrol-pump and fill up with water, Fantas and juice. Maybe sip sweet mint-tea and down a half chicken and salad, before reaching that sprawling camel-changing location. I did, I found a kerosene lit tavern near date-palm trees and parked gratefully.

Night had dropped and only a star-studded bowl above, plus car lights piercing the palms, illuminated this café-cum tea-shop and dormitory combined. Obviously designed for overnight camel caravan teamsters who could never afford anything better. There they were sprawled on high grass-covered beds and inside others sat watching TV and smoking hookers and supping tea. Dreaming their dreams of colourful harems, belly-dancers and pretty boys.

Being almost an Arab, except for my persistent white skin (I'd been resident for five years), I slunk past the crowded forecourt and sat on the one vacant seat at the back where hung an oil-lamp, rather perilously I remember: one of three that lit this mysterious magical place. A mixture of expansive freedom, fear of the unknown and anticipation seemed to pervade this place.

Arabia fascinated me ever since disgorging from a TWA VC10 five years before on Jiddah International airport. We were fumigated by a soft treading tall Arab, clad in a white thobe and turban which covered all except his face from the sun. He walked and squirted with such nonchalant dignity, poise and élan; so that cultivated Arabs have been for me a background of role-models very difficult to emulate in the UK today. No one in Western society can approach them for dignity mixed with humility.

This was a revelation of unimaginable consequence to me at that time. Since living with them I've had my doubts and certainties cooked into a casserole of ideas about myself and the country that spawned me, which has changed my life completely from what it might have been. And as I sat waiting a little impatiently for a glass of mint tea, another event came to consolidate my utter faith in the unexpected being more than likely, rather than the planned expectancy. So be prepared . . . and be resilient and adaptable at all times. I reminded myself.

Two pure white donkeys suddenly appeared near the reed-beds and nuzzled for food. None was given. Instead, the proprietor, an evil looking man, crashed a heavy club down hard on both in fiendish delight, and with furious energy. Both scarpered as fast as four hoofs could go. Two minutes later they reappeared as though joined in conspiracy. Up went their hind hoofs under the nearest frail beds and tables. Then the next ones and so on. Pandemonium ensued. A lamp smashed to the floor. Men swore by the beard of the prophet to castrate, then cut the throats of the offending quadrupeds. Dreadful spells were cast upon their ancestors and future offspring from such as they. Arabs are not known for their equanimity in moments such as this.

Sensing that a frantic search for them would ensue and that unless they'd made good their escape they would be cut up and in the pot or beaten to death, I journeyed on to

d

Yambo, where I slept comfortably in my car. This town was a pre-frontier check-point, where documents are scrutinised and custom payments made. At ten in the morning I sat on a stone step of a small mosque awaiting my turn. A tall cultivated Arab, quite elderly, approached and sat next to me. He was dressed well and spoke reasonable English. He took my arm then my hand warmly and put his other round my shoulders. Looking at my fingernails he remarked in a kind voice that they were not clean and that being an educated man I should remember to clean my body everywhere each day. No one had ever taken that much interest in me in so brief a time, and I didn't know quite how to respond to such human inquisitiveness. I couldn't very well explain I'd had trouble with my carburettors the day before and hadn't showered for twenty-four hours. Like any Englishman I felt a little unsure of his warmth and was relieved when my turn came and I passed through customs intact.

On the far side stood a group of soldiers, a few more cars and some ancient lorries, loaded with sacks of grain and Arabs sitting on top. I had learned earlier that one had to join a caravan of vehicles led by a hired guide, who knew how to traverse the unmettled expanse across ten k's of no-mans' desert. This as a barrier to prevent tanks if ever they invaded from Jordan or Iraq in the north. Other Europeans were in my position and so soon a bargain was struck. The guide came in my car. We each paid a portion of the fee.

We were stopped by soldiers who demanded a free ride to Jordan. I said, "Sorry, I'm loaded already." The one who asked looked angry so I slammed off, hoping not to be shot at. The others caught up later and we traversed this sandy waste with some risks.

Suddenly the guide said, "Imshi imshi affendi," which

means; go go faster. I stepped on it and then there was such a crash. We'd jumped a large-sized ditch and my Akai tape-recorder landed with a crunch on the front bonnet, then slid onto the desert. No damage, so I strapped it more securely. I had to take another car in tow as the radiator was damaged by a similar crash. Finally I cut free as my own wheels were churning into the soft sand. A Land Rover took on the rescue attempt from me.

At Allepo our guide dropped off and I crossed safely into Jordan where the road was very good. I arrived at Amman, found an international youth-hostel, cooked a splendid supper and turned in.

The day's adventures I recollected in my imagination and I began to wonder why life seems to be composed of so many bits and pieces . . . unfinished experiences, or so it seems to my peripatetic nature. I never stay long enough or talk well enough to get close to people. I even began to feel nostalgia for the old Arab gentleman who had been so friendly and at the same time dignified, and though warm and affectionate, was at the same time restrained, showing complete composure and inner-confidence. My haste to quit his company, I analysed before dropping off, was the usual prudish almost sterile reaction, to anyone making a civilised effort at mutual rapport, by Mr Average Englishman, being abroad out of his own dog-kennel. With these sex-starved and despairing images, the phenomenon of sleep came, the mystery of which, even my Saudi adventures failed to unravel.

5

Island Soup

1

"Eh look Horst! There's Harold back again for the high season." Jezebel pointed at his white VW and spoke loudly into her second husband's ear as the big Opel bumped across the Playa del Ingles (English Beach) in the South of Las Palmas holiday island. One of the Canary Islands.

"Yes I see, he's bound to be looking for work as usual. I've got some urgent repairs for him in the Kontiki. I hope he hasn't lost his touch to do restaurant jobs!" exclaimed Horst Schnieder, as he turned to look at his Italian wife.

Young Johan, their eleven-year-old son in the back seat pushed his snub nose against the window and saw the keep fit groups already going through their routines. He heard the leader shouting. "One two three . . . One two three, jump higher much higher . . ."

Johan felt . . . out of it . . . a bit lonely now, so he cuddled Sugar, the lady-dog. Alsation mascot of the Kontiki restaurant and fierce guard-dog, assisting Eric at night.

He fondled her passionately and looked longingly to the fresh morning washed sands, the handsome gymnasts and the vast Atlantic beyond. All so tempting to a young boy trapped inside his dad's new German saloon.

"Put the lead on Sugar before we cross to the Kontiki Johan," Jezebel his step-mother commanded.

Harold, the old English hippy, had parked where he could get water and take a free shower as well as take a gander at the holidaying gymnasts moving their well-oiled bodies in rhythmic unison to the leader's count. Now he threw the ball at the circular group's legs. "Higher, much higher!" He shouted, attracting early bathers before plunging bravely into the choppy ocean as it washed and smoothed tirelessly.

There was a banging on his VW.

Harold responded with a, "Hell man! What are you banging for? I'm up all ready." To his usual knocker up . . . a young waiter from the restaurant, going in for the day."

"OK amigo mio," he rang out, "sorry to disturb you."

Whilst drinking his morning tea Harold regarded the young bronzed beach-boys, already pulling and tugging, carrying four beds (camas) at once. They swore at each other in ringing Spanish colloquialisms, as they spread them neatly side by side safe from the high tide.

He pondered his mood today. Concerned about body/mind harmony. What would the day yield? He mused, as he watched the elegant flight of a few seagulls further south. He puffed at his morning cigarette expansively, as the Opel saloon bounced past over the rough cindered lot.

The arrival of Horst and family registered sluggishly, not as sharply as the howling wind on shore from Morocco, like an angry Muslim ambassador displeased with 'Christian materialism'.

Nothing pressing or important on his personal agenda for this Saturday in late September, so he observed his German restaurant boss with Italian wife and sweet young Johan.

"Thank god for my restaurant and Las Palmas," Horst said to himself, as the car braked two hundred metres beyond Harold.

Johan, the issue from his first matrimony, back on the bank of the Elbe in east Germany, and Sugar his pal, raced off across the dunes, which dimpled, checked and smoothed themselves in a seven-mile long natural embrace of this otherwise rocky coast-line of 'The Island of Love'.

"Wish I had the energy and high spirits to run like him!" said Jezebel wistfully.

"Ja meine frau, that cannot be, you are past it now."

Smiling her agreement but wincing inwardly, she turned to him, closing up with a gentle slam.

"You've changed such a lot since we took the Kontiki," she said pityingly. She looked at him with big black Italian eyes . . . big, black and passionate . . . An artistic woman: her whole face involved. Engaged in a challenging whimsy of desire mixed with a pugnacious scowl of contempt. No subtlety between. Nor should there be any compromise between art and what a real artist discovers about life. And life for her – a constant battle of wits: her's and Horst's wishes, desires, hopes and ambitions for their son and the business against the rest . . .

They started across the cool limpid sand plucking at their sandalled feet. The Kontiki, number three down the line of fourteen identical monstrosities, skirting the majestic embrace of the Atlantic which eternally reproached their sharp cornered, modern presence with its mercurial accommodations.

He sweated in his white dungarees and she looked so cool and attractive in a simple floral skirt and tight tee-shirt showing the contours of her ample breasts and setting off the lustre of her black curls. Obviously she dressed artistically to please herself. Like all genuine taste her style pleased everyone and although business and money were important, she pleased her own gay extravagant self.

They'd made a fortune in the last three years, pandering to the tastes, whimsies and predilections in food, drink and decor for tourists. Parties, banquets, barbeques arranged at night for rich Swedes, Danes, Dutch and American clients.

Horst no longer looked at how she dressed. He sought young delights in Las Palmas city, fifty kilometres away, on his days off.

As though reading Horst's thoughts, she took his hand as in their courtship and squeezing gently, she questioned, "Why don't you get Harold to make a gaily painted wind-wheel, like his over there, fixed above the entrance? Bring in the kids with their mums and dads. That's what's wanted . . . competition's fiercer every day! Give 'em gimmicks, amusements! People bent on pleasure expect life to feed their fantasies. Encouraged to be personally, even intimately related, like visiting old friends."

"OK I'll ask him to make one. I agree he's good but we've not paid him for the diesel repair or the rustic menu notices burnt into natural pine, which he hung on chains from the ceiling, remember!"

"That's what I say. He's handy . . . makes the place a little more human . . . not so much like a rip-off joint!"

They stopped half way across, to admire the sky just changing from clear blue to liquid golden orange as the sun rose over the highest peak, casting brilliant light on Harold's wind-wheel blades turning slower now, as the wind subsided.

Horst turned to her with his usual impassive podgy-faced look, and said, "Alright we must bait the hook carefully. I trust your judgement in matters of running the business.

Let's have him over for breakfast . . . a special breakfast tomorrow, before I ask him to work for us. There's the gas-lines, and Carlos reported the potato-machine motor has packed up again, spatulas, frying-pan handles, even though he needs the money, you know how obstinate and independent he is. Better still; here, take the keys to the till, stock and beer-fridge. Eric will be up now and I see the chef and boys going in. You go on. I'll butter him up now. He's up shaving, I saw as we passed in the car. He'll be drinking his morning poison . . . thick tea soup which all Limeys like. It's still early, perhaps I can get him on with it. The wind-wheel, I mean – right away."

So, turning abruptly, he strode towards Harold's mobile electricity producing wind-powered sculpture.

"Don't forget to pay him for the jobs he did last year," she cried after him into the wind, as he lumbered heavily over a steep bush-covered dune.

Switching direction he moved swiftly to his car. Strange! For after a decision he rarely changed, but instinctive low cunning now dictated at least a semblance of friendship and in turn that demanded form, style, even a show of protocol between two former enemies. Even if, as was becoming clear, their several interests drew them uncomfortably into each other's survival orbit of existence. Harold the poet artisan, and Horst Schnieder, a ruthless businessman!

He drove swiftly to his new villa (gardens and swimming pool still in progress by strong local peasants,) which overlooked the Maspalomas lighthouse on the razor rocks four kilometres from Playa Ingles. The villa was sited on a fifty metre high plateaux, giving the Schnieders the finest seascape views on the whole island.

Proudly, he remembered escaping from his Gasthauser (Guest-house) on the banks of the Elbe. East German tax-

Inspectors were carefully examining his returns, fraudulently and expertly done by a corrupt accountant, who had spent alternate weekends there cooking the books and having an affair with Eric, Horst's one-time boyfriend. Eric played butch with both men, showing how versatile he was. He'd deserted his young German wife and son to join Horst in his restaurant adventure as his personal assistant.

"Yes!" he thought looking out. "A very good buy that old American wind-pump. I bought it for peanuts off a tomato grower, who was forced to close for lack of water." The water-table lowered each year as it was syphoned to Maspalomas new town. "Harold did a good job on that too." His thoughts raced . . . but were self-centred.

He never reflected on the way tourism radically changed the lives of the Islanders. Tourists showered five times per day and tomato-growers unable to survive in the south. He noted with pleasure that Harold had set the frame of the mill in deep concrete. Still the same blades, welded solidly to an outer rim, cleverly adapted to pump water for domestic use from the artesian well. By moving a gear-shift, it disengaged and drove an alternator, producing current for his home, provided the wind blew. For emergencies he had another noisy smelly diesel-generator.

He shouted Antonia from the battery-shed. No answer! He noted the batteries well up. She'd gone shopping, so he scribbled a message in Spanish, demanding supper to be served on the patio facing south-west. Placed it on top of the new infra-red cooker, dived into his bed-chamber, kicked the cat off his pillow, and changed into his leather shorts (lederhosen) and clean mauve sweat-shirt with his own, bold insignia – a Kontiki raft on a smooth idyllic azure sea – all in natural colours, within a nine-inch circle, displayed on his chest.

Two minutes later he was in the Land Rover. This time rolling slowly past the workmen busy planting young palm trees, mimosa and hibiscus. Miguel and David were getting on with the swimming pool (das schimm bassin) his latest status-symbol. He picked up speed, returning to the beach just as Harold finished his latest poem. Well, 'verses' he called them. Tried to catch in words those eternal moments we all experience. He replaced his biro, lit a fag and wondered what the current scene would yield? Maybe a little inspiration today! Or he'd go in for a dip first and enjoy that sharp healthy feeling he loved so much. A kind of physical song of the flesh in harmony with the bitter sweet awareness of life in all its sadness, joy and aspiration.

Those beautiful hippies seen last year! Mostly young randy holidaying Americans, Swedes, Germans and a few Brits. All from affluent homes, clad in scanty shorts and looking so fit, bronzed and at one with nature. Not as hardy, tough and resilient though as Juan, Miguel and Pedro. All local beach-boys whom he could see from here. Poor mostly, hard working and cheerful as the island sun. And Juan, his favourite, as perfectly formed as ever his old crafty eyes had seen. All being a virile combination of fine Guanche blood, a benevolent climate, and the rest: sheer hard graft, looking after the animal-comforts of the rich visitors.

Yes, he thought. Seeing the connection.

POVERTY
What lessons God teaches to those who're poor!
Gratitude for a crust of bread
A cup of wine a benefice, a plate of meat divine . . .

What careful minds who make of want, philosophy . . .

Learning to care with true economy
Resourceful use and patient thrift
Makes perfect how to give and spend
When others' needs dictate a portion of one's small estate . . .

For saving, short of giving, is a niggard's state
Ending in misers' dreams, provoked by avarice
Thus sufficient to himself in all . . .
But he who gives, is all to all
Who stumble in this world and fall.

"There now, that'll af't do," emphasising his factory-style Lancashire accent, because he had solidarity and felt at one with his unsuspecting friends on the beach below. Already they sweated at their tasks as the semi-tropical sun rose and bus-loads of tourists arrived. They wandered into bars or walked picky and choosey down the long rows of colourful parasols (sun-shades) and camas (beach-beds) till they were seduced with the charms of these suave, attractively robust locals.

Others splashed lazily in the shallows. Harold noted that quite a number went on their way to a remote point south, where a well-known nude bathing stretch lay.

Then, as though expecting a visitor, Harold washed up the breakfast plate and tea-mug . . . tidied round . . . lit a fag, and placed his poetry book carefully on the shelf. He scrambled into tight white trunks and feeling fresh and healthy, examined his hand-made wind charger. An old alternator recycled from a derelict car, fitted to four blades made from driftwood.

"Too much wind! I'll increase the angle of attack." After this operation Horst's Rover skidded to a halt next to his waterless camel (tiny VW station-wagon) which he'd lived and travelled in since leaving Saudi Arabia, four years ago.

He loved teaching English there but found the political environment tough to digest without cultural diarrhoea or 'culture shock' as ex-patriot teachers described it.

Jeddah was a hot-bed of Muslim revisionists, mixed with CIA agents, KGB infiltrators, Christian do-gooders, militant capitalist entrepreneurs, homosexual school-teachers (like himself); Italian, German and Swedish civil engineers, re-building the city, two new airports plus schools, universities and telecommunications; dispossessed Palestinian teachers stirring it up in the class-rooms, about Israelis stealing Arab lands on the basis that the Bible promised the Jews a permanent paradise, provided they kept the Holy Covenant with God. Of course anathema to devout Muslims who read the Koran and followed Mohammed.

Then there were South Yemenies getting through on phony pilgrim trips to Mecca, nearby, trying to convert everyone to Communism. Oil-rich Sheiks, returning from Europe with ultra-modern ideas: "Quite a stew-pot, and as usual, when the pot boils, much scum surfaces." Thought Harold ruefully as he reflected upon his time spent there.

So now, here in Las Palmas, on this marvellous beach, now desecrated and turned into a commercial tourist tip, Harold was unusually alert to the effects of modern-style colonialism dressed as tourism, and the sale of the best beaches and strips of land to big commercial building companies.

Decision makers fashioning our future environment. Manipulating manners and forming habits difficult to throw off. Changing the nature of existence for the proud descendants of the ancient Guanche traditions of Nature worship (as practised before Christopher Columbus won the Island for Metropolitan Spain). Even changing their genuine

Catholic beliefs, ingeniously woven into the old Guanche culture.

Because of this modern ferment in Saudi Arabia and Las Palmas, conflicting with ancient ways, Harold was ill-disposed towards tourists and 'get rich quick' business people.

However, he'd known Horst and his wife for three years, off and on his annual visits, made mostly in the high season, so he tried to be friendly whilst engaged in work-schedules with them both. "Culturally though, the battle is still on. My values and interests against yours, you money-grubbing exploiting bastard." He said, under his breath. "And what about last year's work? Six thousand pesetas you owe me." Also under his breath.

When the Land Rover stopped, Harold was in a decidedly diffident, not to say ambivalent mood, towards employers of any sort, let alone an ex-Nazi-cum-opportunist restauranteur, from the Elbe valley in Northern Prussia.

What would you do if you were surrounded with beautiful scenery, rolling breakers thundering up the beach, the most gorgeous boys and girls walking about like Greek gods and goddesses, filling you with aesthetic thoughts and the desires that follow, and then (because of survival) you are forced to engage with a man who hasn't seen his own penis for the last five years because his stomach bulges over his leather shorts like a blown-up pig's bladder?

Harold was fond of asking difficult questions addressed to the wild wind and straggling beach. Then for a change he asked himself out loud a serious question.

"What is my spiritual situation . . . the condition of my soul in the last quarter of this turbulent century?"

"Why does one have to tolerate ugliness in order to honour beauty?"

"Why submit to money-motivation, when life is a mysterious pilgrimage of personal and universal discovery of truth?"

Harold felt his higher self (not always alert) outraged. As form, styled in this life, is a living proof that one believes in it, if not in the next. Harold was sufficiently sceptical to know that those who refuse to honour noble precepts, beauties and part-perfections we see on mother earth, are not likely to honour them in the next. Gross people were by definition against all aesthetic and poetic values, and if not to be judged obscene, then to be adroitly dealt with.

Why this show of affluence though? . . . Clothes changed and in the British built Land Rover? Well, of course, he had to bring stores across the deep sandy waste-land to his Kontiki didn't he!

"Hola amigo! Das mus die leicht machine, ja?"

"Yes it is. Do you like it?"

"Ja, it is goot verking."

"Costs nothing to charge battery. I can stay for months and start OK."

"Why not patent it?"

"It isn't compact enough and in any case, I'm a wanderer, a scholar-gypsy, not a capitalist businessman like you."

Harold dipped a scrawny arm into his car as though feeling into a lucky dip fair-ground barrel, pulled out a Caballero cigarette and lit it with a soft paper-stemmed match. The feel made him aware of ecology and respect for all materials. Such cheap ones made from paper soaked in tallow. The only snag; one had to grip them near the head to strike. Could be made in a self-sufficient community, when in future he would try to join others to establish a little bit of heaven on earth . . . at the end of his pilgrimage through the mortal coil. There's no chance of saying no to capitalist modes of doing business on one's own, or of defying the world-wide communist conspiracy, dragooning everyone into mindless conformity. He soliloquised.

Unaware of Harold's private ruminations of capitalism eventually destroying itself and perhaps the world as well, Horst scrambled out of his Rover, Hitched his shorts tight against his big belly, planted his legs firmly as a wrestler ready for a game of 'catch as catch can', with Harold as his protagonist. But in this game, not physical but a game of cunning use of his grasp of Pommy lingo he'd picked up in American and British sectors of Berlin whilst hawking hamburgers, chips and ice-cream to GIs and Tommies, before making his pile on the Elbe and escaping from the Russian controlled East.

"Nice to see you back again. My wife is very fed-ups! Too much work. She likes for me and you to go . . . look at Cape Verde Island, once Portuguese, now independent. Make aerial survey for best beach location, then buy land . . . make private aerodrome . . . build holiday compound for whites only and inside a pleasure and leisure layout for rich clients. All built by real blackies. Much cheaper than these jumped up Guanche white niggers: getting uppity about pay, holidays and working-conditions these days."

Harold's hackles rose. He couldn't stand such verbal attacks against those he loved, the happy-go-lucky indigenous locals, but he sympathised profoundly with Jezebel, for he knew how hard she worked and that she was a neglected woman. Left to serve the clients and to make money.

So Harold was emotionally confused at this moment . . . (adrenaline feeding his desire to hit the man) . . . he couldn't deal coolly with Horst's suggestion. He looked away to the sea for comfort. Horst continued in the same monotones.

Heavy jowls going like an automat.

"You see now why I take you on such a flight? You are practical. Also your ideas for make electricity very goot over there. What do you say?"

Horst drew a deep breath and leaned against the truck to recover from his sustained linguistic attack. And now with an alert gleam in his piggy eyes, he looked for signs of interest and emotional committal to appear in Harold's mobile face.

The cigarette smoke curled from Harold's lips as he turned calmly to Horst. "It's a great idea," he said diplomatically, "but difficult to realise. That is unless you are rich enough to hire a ship to transport all building materials, machines, tools and bulldozers etc. Plus negotiating purchase of terrain and construction permit from, who knows? Perhaps a tough mafia type bunch runs the show on Cape Verde Island!"

Harold thought it an absurdity, dismissing it and thinking, a very complex character this Kraut. So he continued: "You romance too much! Let's talk of present problems. Why don't you employ me to make a big wind-charger to produce current for the Kontiki as I did last year up at your Villa?"

"No, too complicated! What will the ayuntamiento (mayor) say? It was difficult enough to renew my concession to operate as it is. I bribed him last year. As you know the Kontiki is on the best site. Then again, what happens on a calm day, no current . . ?"

"Easy! Have your diesel in reserve. Simple . . . save money, no awful smell or noise . . . staff healthier and happier, make more profit from discerning clients." As though to add emphasis to his remarks, two diesels from beach cafés started chugging and thudding their noisy routine. Others join soon till the beach reverberates with our century's major contribution to international culture, a terrible technical 'Punk music' of pitiless monotony.

"Well yes, you are probably right, Harold! I'll think about it, but right now watch the tourist coaches pulling in to the lot. Rich Danskies, Swedes and Yankees. Watch where they go when they've sorted themselves out! You see them . . . after a stuffy coach-trip they want cool drinks, ice-cream, coffee and a cigarette. So many go in the Pedro bar and don't see my Kontiki until lunch when I do well, as you know."

"Why not fix a great totem pole outside with a hand carved relief showing hearty Guanche peasants loving in three dimensional action?" Harold laughingly suggested with a touch of malice in his teacher's voice. He knew that false values of money motivated folk never allowed them to use their imagination beyond narrow views of what moral proprieties consisted of. Overt open sexual pleasure? No, never. Hide it, let it be masturbated away down the lavatory pan in unhealthy fantasy. But unscrupulous money making? Quite good, quite acceptable and much less dangerous to the status quo than free love. Homely peters and fertile yearning vaginas, redeemed of filthy lucre were, to Harold's poetic soul, perfectly acceptable and never obscene. For him money-worship was vastly inferior to phallic, or, as he put it 'clean peters'.

"That'd bring 'em in," he continued, "if that's all you're interested in, PROFIT . . . !"

Horst tried without success to cover his feelings of having lost this verbal battle. Harold knew he'd bitten hard.

"Have to go now. She's expecting me," he said soberly. "Eric is on top repairing the water tank. Only her chef and young Pablo to serve. He backed towards the Land Rover, then said, "What about making a fun windmill for decoration, painted psychedelically, spots picking it out at night, coloured lights round the roof?"

How to reconcile the irreconcilable? Harold asked the hot barren sands beneath his sandals. How do you make human the totally inhuman equation? No use wasting any more breath talking ecology to such as he. "What about the money. That bill you owe me from last year. Six thousand pesetas?"

"Yes, OK, come for breakfast tomorrow. Bring the accounts and we'll sort things out. Meanwhile Jezebel would like a fun windmill on top. Are you keen?"

Difficult for Harold . . . he needed work badly just to survive in this competitive hell. He shouted over as Horst switched the ignition. "OK, I'll do a sketch: tail-fin and six coloured blades on steel shaft with roller bearings tomorrow. That'd be the best I can do for JEZEBEL," he emphasised. Next he grabbed a blood-red towel, stuck his feet into home-made tyre-soled sandals and shoved a battered straw hat on his greying head whilst Horst's Rover wheels spat out spumes of silvery sand from the defeated yet stubborn dunes, as he drove erratically to the Kontiki.

With his brown legs thrusting out of tiny shorts, a sketch block, soft 11B pencil, eraser, towel and comb stuffed into a plastic bag, Harold wended his way in the shallows to the Kontiki.

After his devious entente with Horst his mood changed to optimism. What with a clear sky and an inviting wave-washed beach and the prospect of earning a little money and maybe a settlement of last year's wages for work done up at the new Villa, and now the chance of a chat and a drink in the Kontiki before sketching and having that swim he'd promised himself, despondency lifted; as on a misty morn before and after the sun transforms this island (of mysterious volcanic activity) from darkest geology, to a playground for the frivolous humans who will walk its beaches as though kings of all, instead of the microbes that we are against such eternity here present.

"Hello Eric. Good morning to you!"

"Hi, what's cooking with you today?"

"Oh nothing startling, Eric. Loads of tourists arriving as usual. You'll be run off your feet 'ere long me jolly boy. Give's a packet of fags . . . Caballeros . . . and a Gold-label please."

"Sure, I'll have one with you." They drank up.

Harold took his leave, as Eric seemed a little distant, not himself today.

He wandered on and on splashing and enjoying the soft sand squelching through his bare feet, a lovely sensuous feel as the wet sand sucked possessively. Usually he went to the oasis at the tip but today he felt abandoned to his animal desire for (at least in theory) being part of the local scene, however banal. His battered hat wove its way through the lines of prostrate semi-sentient bodies. Some had already taken their first dip and were busily anointing themselves with oil, then replacing their white plastic nose-shields, rendering them utterly insipid and repellant to his thoroughly aroused aesthetic sensibility.

Picking out a well-built lad of about seventeen, who moments before, splashed his boisterous way out of the shallows and plonked himself down: distancing himself from the nearest morass of tubular camp-beds and plastic paraphernalia, that brown-body maniacs consider essential for their first and probably their last fortnight in close contact with Mother Nature.

Harold assumed the young man had basic good taste, for he thought for himself in the event of close contact with the fresh washed sands. He also stretched out gratefully enough

91

and felt the feathers of his poetic soul to grow from such nourishment. And a flowing glowing human presence only metres from him. He ached for contact with human beauty, not knowing, even at his mature age, that beauty is but the depth of skin and only an indication not a reality of life, until proved daily.

He took out his block and instead of drawing a windmill, he drew the handsome shape of the recumbent boy. A human presence that obliterated mundane fears of not surviving in this harsh impersonal world completely from his consciousness.

The handsome lad rested, oblivious of Harold's joy at his present state of 'youth's glad hour', let alone the state of ecstacy that prompted such artistic efforts with block and feverish pencil.

Harold finished sketching in details of physical excellence . . . the Nature God he so ardently worshipped. Only saddened that he had no coloured pencils, so as to put in the golden tints, subtle movements of delicate muscles at lips and eyes as well as abdomen, thighs and groin.

Not a word was spoken, but the boy glanced warmly in his direction . . . knowing he was being admired and celebrated. The ocean pounded its approval of such a silent trysting that has no verbal equivalent.

With a heavy sigh he gave it a final touch, popped it into his plastic bag. Then feeling doubly inspired, he took it out and wrote:

THE BEACH
A boy's eyes lit upon my face
And gave me warmth
Much stronger than the sun
And I, his vassal slave, said, "Cheerio to him".

He left suddenly, saying to himself, "Ah, now for a swim!" Running spiritedly towards the rolling breakers he dived in striking out with powerful strokes.

"What a relief!" As he dived again, against the pull. Out he came. Waved to the young Portuguese in an intimate salute of approval. Then back to the car, to start work on the decorative windmill for the Kontiki.

2

"She's coming on heat, Jez!"

"What d'ye say, Eric? Can't hear you."

"Sugar, the dog," in a louder voice. "She's hot again. Have to keep her locked up for two weeks."

Jezebel swung open the door into the Kontiki as Eric finished cleaning and replacing chairs and tables. He wrung out his mop and looked for a reply from her amorous lips. She nodded assent, as opening the till with her right hand and switching on the stereo with her left she turned to gaze at him.

La Boheme opera music came on loud and clear. (At last a delightful song of Bohemian love much better than the infernal diesel.) She continued to watch Eric as he enticed Sugar with a chicken-bone, attaching her deftly to the bar-rail with a life-belt cord hanging near the prices on his right.

"Safe until Johan takes her for a swim," Eric said, as he did table-settings, with red napkins tucked into each wine glass.

"Eric my love, be a dear and take coffee, hamburgers, rolls and marmalade to Harold and Horst at the back. I've set the table, and now they're arguing about money . . . bills from last year!"

"Right away, Jez. Include butter and sugar as usual?"

"Yes please!"

He felt her eyes upon him, so he showily heaved a couple of crates of empties on to his shoulder and dumped them for the dray-man before taking the big tray of eats round to Harold and Horst.

A little mist (portent of a heavy sultry atmosphere) shrouded the beach at this early breakfast-time as Horst read through Harold's list.

"What is this . . . Repair of ice-cream vacuum flask container, one hundred pesetas?" Eric heard as he laid out the food. Horst was angry. His finger trembled on the annotated list of work done. Harold replied calmly.

"It is correct. It took four hours to repair. Also I took your work-men back and to the Villa from the beach several times and have not charged. Anyway, if you don't agree, just pay me what you would pay yourself for the same work."

As he said this he looked steadily into the eyes of the big boss. He looked away; broke the trance and was about to take a sip of coffee. Suddenly the table caught him in the groin. He doubled up. His glasses dropped on to the sand, then flailing fists came from all angles and he decided to run.

Horst chased him but to no avail, as Harold was slim and wiry and soon out-distanced the stronger man.

His shirt ripped from shoulders and shorts covered with coffee stains, he ran to a safe distance. Then returned to his car.

"What a bloody man!" He said to the warming air. "Did the work as cheaply as I could and now he won't pay an honest bill. Where's my Aspros?"

He went over to the big Mercedes and asked Peter (Pedro as he preferred), "Have you got a headache pill please?"

"What's this! What the devil has happened to you?" he asked in sympathetic tones.

"Oh a dust-up with Horst about payment! He hasn't paid for work I did last year."

"Never mind! I'll go across with you next time and ask Jezebel to hand over. Have a cup of tea and here, take two of these," he said, handing Harold a couple of aspirins. "Then rest a while. You'll soon be OK again," he finished reassuringly.

Horst swept off wildly in the Land Rover. His usual trip to Las Palmas in order to buy provisions and find a bit of fresh skirt for himself.

Back at the restaurant, Eric returned to his bar-room duties and Jezebel demanded to know the whole story. He supplied her with the facts then passed close-by, disappearing to help Pablo and Carlos the chef prepare for the day's hectic struggle with heat, gas-leaks, diesel-fumes, noise and confined space in the kitchen, where occasional furious trade-winds blew as though a Moroccan Muslim Ayatollah had declared war on Europeans. These winds intruded sand right into their food so carefully prepared, if they didn't watch out and close all windows doors and crevices.

Jezebel filled with ardour . . . a sudden desire for the life she knew rested in Eric's groin, and which he could give if he so wished. How could she get him to wish though? She hadn't much to offer a young man in looks perhaps, but in motherly appeal and worldliness, few women were her equal, and she knew this as well as she knew her young step-son Johan. But Eric! . . .So unpredictable!

He passed close, carrying a sack of potatoes.

So different to Horst! as she followed, eyeing everything about him. Refreshing her memory intensely, making desire painful to bear (unless consummated) as she gazed furtively at his lithe legs (free except for trunks) his narrow, tanned torso, lively crotch, shaggy face, blue eyes, dancing mischievously beneath his humorous straw-thatch.

Much more dynamic and sensual than Horst, she thought. Feeling glad as she shouted a sonorous " 'Ci ci'" to the chef, who'd asked her: "Has the water-tanker been to fill up for the week?"

Suddenly and spontaneously she embraced Eric round the midriff. Squeezing gently above his hips. Enough to titillate his hormones. Soothing him for the day she hoped; for, isn't he well-fed, young, sexy and as bad-tempered as a Spanish bull on the run in Pamplona, if he becomes too frustrated? And I know how demanding his job is, she reflected.

She served two young girls with ice-cream cornets. Her thoughts raced: How glad she was that this strong young German guarded the Kontiki at night. She didn't really care if he did lure girls into the bar as long as business was finished for the day. She was only sad that she was not the one he loved!

Anyway, it made her feel young again. She remembered Horst bringing him to their 'Alpine Hotel' outside Wittenberge, whilst on the run from his wife, a few years since.

She spoke in flat practical tones to the chef.

"Carlos, tell Pablo to help Eric to stack the empties and gas-cylinders ready for the Land Rover when Horst returns. Then you are to prepare salads

"Fifty mixed, fifty tomato, twenty-five green with onion . . . de-frost the usual fish, meat, fruit and veg, five kilos hamburgers, don't forget eggs and Pablo, start peeling potatoes! The machine is broken.

"Johan! A job for you too. Take these broken spatulas and

frying-pan handles to Harold for repairs. We don't want any accidents! Tell him I'll square up the accounts with him . . . The bills Horst got angry about. He will understand."

"Can I have a 'treat' bar mother?"

"Yes, when you've done your errands and not before."

Carlos gave his usual sunshine boyish grin of accord as he dexterously flipped a sizzling beef-burger, pressing it vigorously on the hot-plate. A first order out of hundreds before knocking off at six, when his brother Miguel would take over. He saved his breath to battle with the foeted sand blowing in, and the diesel noise.

Pablo had already started on the mountain of spuds but stuck his knife into a big one and helped the others stack the heavy crates and cylinders. "Look out Pablo!" shouted Eric as a top crate almost landed in the deepfry chip-unit. As it was, a bottle did fall in and they were splashed with hot oil. All too close and difficult to negotiate even without crates on their shoulders.

Fernando, the dish-wash porter, steadied him up and helped the still adolescent boy to stow full bottles of Schweppes bitter lemon and orange into the bar-fridges without rupturing himself. Unconsciously they supported each other from the deep roots of their common heritage when difficulties arose. Next they polished off the tables, bar-room, floors and set the tables, chairs and parasols, neatly side by side outside, to give maximum view and free air-flow to the clients. For, when the temperature soars into the nineties, about ten-thirty, cool dips and iced-drinks are the orders for the day.

"Come on you guys! Stop arsing around," Eric entreated, as odd clients came tripping into the bar.

"Salads to cut: and the chef needs help on the hotplate."

"OK. Don't get up-tight like the big boss Eric. We're

doing our best," retorted Pablo, as he lifted young Johan onto his shoulders and marched inside, in a playful mood.

Johan was hot and hungry so he too was soon served when a lull showed.

Johan had the weekend off school, so he missed his school pals, and he'd just returned from a trip to watch the fishermen pull in and land their catch. A fascinating sight!

"Club-sandwich and a peach Melba please, Eric!" His mother was busy again with tourists, so Eric gave him an extra big one.

"Have you taken the spatulas over to Harold?" demanded Eric.

"No, not yet. He's had a fight with my dad, and he's resting up I think . . . not taken his tools out. So I watched the boats. Don't tell Ma will you!"

"OK. Take them over to him when he gets up."

Johan dug his strong white teeth into the melange of onions, bread, beef and mustard.

Sugar barked furiously to be released, straining at her captive rope. She loved him almost like his step-mother, whom she adored. Now though it was cupboard-love, for as soon as Eric released her, she scampered across to where Johan sat and placed a demanding paw on his bare left thigh. Cocking her head on one side and fixing him with her wise canine eyes, which he couldn't resist. He looked to see if his mother was watching and promptly gave Sugar a chunk of his sandwich.

"Come . . . Come on Sugar! Let's go and see old Harold." They chased each other across the no-man's-land of burning sand to Harold's wind-wheel: always turning and veering with the wind . . . off-shore in the early morn and on-shore by midday.

Harold had had a good rest and was up now near the VW,

back bent, working on a small portable table.

Sugar lazily inspected the pile of rocks (securing the vertical shaft upon which the propeller shaft and fin was set) and anointed one with her pee . . . just in case.

"Mum says can you repair these things?" As he placed them on the table.

Harold rested his saw, looked up slowly from the wind-wheel blades he was hand-crafting, and saw an angel clothed in human flesh, about four-foot nothing. Tousled blond hair, snub-nose, hazel eyes, same as Horst's. But so vital . . . innocent and engaging at the same time, set into a face that should have been a girl's, but for the obviously male body clearly defined in miniature proportions.

"Can't exactly say for today but I'll promise to repair them by tomorrow, when I'll be measuring up for the girder-post for the mill. Tell your step-Mum I'll put the costs onto the old bill, then she can pay when she's ready." Harold pulled on Sugar's leash as she nosed into his butter, the rear hatch having blown open with a sudden gust of wind.

"Yes, OK Harold. Mother said she will pay you. Do you like fish?"

"Sure, especially merlusa." (Hake)

"Then go quickly to that boat over there. They caught a lot of sardines, maybe there's some left." He pointed excitedly, way out east.

"OK, young man, thank you for the tip."

"It is alright Harold. I hope you are better now. Bye Bye! See you soon."

Since early adolescence, Harold always tried, whatever the difficulties, to communicate his inner feelings to those who excited them. Thinking this to be the only civilised way of dealing with emotions. But about the Island as a whole: Well, it represented so much natural beauty . . . at least the undeveloped quiet places . . . a sensuous paradise of ever-changing shapes, textures and atmospheres. Sandy beaches, (one or two still unpolluted with oil-slicks or plastic rubbish) when hot at midday, induced a feeling of guilt in those who trespassed over virgin land. Then a benevolent forgiveness when cool at night. And the hills and deep ravines (mostly dried up) and soft lower slopes, green, fertile and shady, all intoxicated a would-be sensualist. Then the close presence of this perfectly built German boy . . . The son of a North Prussian frog-man, hand-picked by Herr Hitler. Horst must have been a perfectly malleable 'fighting machine', to be picked out by Adolf in nineteen thirty-six. How he had deteriorated though since then. Did his beautiful son Johan represent a kind of redemption of his warring years, or was his son Nature's reproach?

No such problematic questioning occurred to Harold though about physical beauty. It was simply and always divine revelation . . . for it always startled him into realms of the purest. His immediate reactions didn't always accord with the proprieties. So, quite often, Harold found his finest inspirations confounded by contemporary prejudice.

Thus it had to be . . . a life, not totally sublimated (for there had been occasions for intimate endearment) but nearly so. No matter, he enjoyed feelings of inner harmony by seeing and appreciating, rather than possessing!

Always optimistic that he might encounter agreeable friends, Harold ran off up the beach to buy fish, just in case! And Johan, who had by now delivered Harold's message to his mother, stood doodling outside. Then he straightened up and watched with growing curiosity, as a grey saloon Ford rolled to a stop almost next to Harold's work-bench.

Two young Americans climbed out. One big and blond the other slim but strong looking. As he looked on, they unrolled a green ridge-tent and quickly erected it.

He played with Sugar. Throwing a big thigh-bone into the dusty dunes, whilst she barked and frisked in high glee. Then he attached her to the supply-shed. Placed left-overs and half a gallon of water in a handleless saucepan for his favourite.

Cuddling her once more before leaving, she jumped up, licking him passionately inside his left ear and giving him ecstatic feelings of physical delight. The diesel noise, swirling sand, and Sugar's passionate kiss, exciting in him the first stirrings of his healthy animal nature.

He didn't know quite what to do as he felt himself going hard, but Sugar knew and licked him again on his navel.

So he left her in the dark, noisy, smelly shed and ran and ran in strong wind and brilliant light across the hard sand, until, almost breathless, he dived, but only when forced as his legs were embraced in the sensuous suck and pluck of the heavy tidal wash.

Striking out for Morocco, he felt exhilarated: well able to master the rolling swell some thirty metres out from the surf-washed beach. How he enjoyed these weekends and half-term holidays away from the city. Everywhere open, invitingly mysterious and free. The Island loved him in return as one of her own and was shaping him to her own exquisite mould. Island voices: potent . . . and benevolent to those she loved. Giving her own strength and beauty to those who protected her quiet places. For how much longer? No one knew. For already her beauty was threatened. Hills, valleys, shores, beaches, desecrated with tourist trivia: oil slicks and her skies adulterated with burning plastic debris from the tourist supermarket packaging. The whisperings that had sustained generation after generation may soon cease!

A surf-board, piloted by a big bronzed man with a Roman nose, raced past him. White glistening decks, orange coloured sail, whipping and snapping disagreeably in the fresh on-shore breeze.

The man smiled at Johan directly, so he struck out with bolder strokes. He waved back as a big one thundered in, making him gasp as he struggled against its pull.

Now, two boys are swimming towards him. He recognises them as the Americans. They swing a white beach-ball between them. Vigorously turning from back to side then breast or crawl like versatile young porpoises, racing each other when free of the ball. It splashed into his eyes in a salty spray, bouncing away from his grasp. Without a word he returned it expertly to the blond lad with the fine muscular body and kindly looking blue-grey eyes.

The blond head disappeared and moments later Johan felt strong hands gripping him round his middle. It was a close embrace, warm, friendly and yet demonstratively passionate. Johan didn't struggle. After his experience in the supply-shed with Sugar, he needed this.

Like a young faun, he folded himself into the strong boy's grasp. He loved the togetherness feeling so much, like an electric charge shooting through his small but lively and responsive body. Their hands went lower to each other's groins, and the warm water pushed them close with its subtle movement. Unconsciously he needed acceptance, not only from his mother in deeds and words. But like now, by a person of his own sex . . . a strong dominant male whom he could accept as a mythical hero. And Roary, close to manhood, wished to expand: to express his protective and tender feelings just as strongly as any others.

A mountainous wave pushed them even closer as it swept them inwards to the rocks. Conspiring nature made them hold each other tighter still, making them gasp for breath and shout for joy in the sane moment, as she economised on schools of doubtful merit, classical poetry and Renaissance sculptures, teaching her lessons of sensuality more powerfully than the arts of man, thrice removed from the truth.

Johan's boyish world of jet-planes, space-ships, decrepit school-masters and mathematics, was enlarged and illuminated in those few moments of contact without language. Free from the sophisticated torture of the grown-ups.

He felt Roary's body to be so strong. He was secure: self-confident at last with this grown-up lad from the USA, and wished the mood would last for ever. But it was not to be . . . the turbulent ocean saw to that. Suddenly he freed himself and grasped Roary's leg at the top. A bold gesture for a young one, then they parted laughingly and spat salt-water at each other until Roary shouted, "Great isn't it?" In a North American drawl. Familiarly, Johan threw the ball at him and said, "Ja it is very fine, ja ja," in bad English learnt at the German Folk High-School (Junior section) in Las Palmas. Roary Westland from Chicago, sixteen and nearly full grown: willowy and as supple as an Olympic swimmer, loved to hear this smart looking, good-natured European kid. Made him feel grown-up: Europeanised, cultivated more than he knew he was. Like putting on a fresh skin. Different from being just a citizen of stodgy old 'Uncle Sam'.

Roary flipped the ball to Rodney Fletcher. "Say Rod, Can Johan camp out with us tonight?"

"Sure!" he mildly exclaimed. "Tent's big enough for three. Not all built as a young bullock like you. He's kinda small and I'm not that grown-up yet. Enough grub too!"

"We'll have that midnight swim we promised ourselves since arriving on this peanut-sized European playground. Then cook some spuds on an open camp-fire. Roast 'em eh? What do you say, the both of you?"

His voice, almost a man's, sounded in excitement at arranging his first ever supper for a newly acquired foreign guy. Plans ran through his head as strong as the ocean. Suddenly life was important . . . dynamic. They weren't just tourists, they were tribal-chiefs, real allies for a time if not 'life-long buddies'.

Travellers of the world, discovering its emotional riches as well as its evocative sights, sounds, smells, foods and drinks.

"OK by me!" Roary replied enthusiastically. "How about you, Johan?"

"Ja, that is good, I ask my Mutter: Just make for OK by her. Come, let's go ashore! I'll get Cokes for you both in my mum's restaurant."

They raced past other kids, old dears and dainty timid people just popping a toe in as the surfer swooped in onto the beach on the crest of a breaker. They kicked water into each others' ear-holes. Johan jumped onto Roary's back shouting a vulgar German phrase of the (come on let's fight) pugnacious variety. Roary flung him off. Landing Johan in the shallows in a final baptism of having swam together as new-found friends. Then they chased off . . . full speed for the Kontiki. With chest stuck out proudly, straw thatch askew, hazel eyes alert and big as antelopes, small bum tight and compact in his white slip-on jockeys, he thrust his strong body through the tourist crowd, down the middle of the tables to his mum at the till.

"Three iced Cokes, bitte!" She looked up sharply. Her humorous mouth slightly open . . . anxious eyes, lively and friendly, taking in every detail of the total scene.

She liked what she saw much more than she dared show. So different, these hippies, to the dreary tourists. She stopped half way from giving change to a close-cropped military type. A one time comrade of Horst's in Hitler's army, now retired and on holiday, named Peter (Pedro, as he preferred to identify with the Island people, who were gentle and loved to make music), and forgetting his former SS days in Rommel's Panzar tank-unit.

Horst and he were about the same age and had met in the Italian campaign, where Horst met his present wife Jezebel.

Pedro gave the young boy a worldly glance of appraisal and his step-mum an encouraging grin.

She put the change into the big man's hand and said almost in a whispered intrigue, "Isn't he pretty!" Slanting her eyes past Pedro (Peter) to the clear glass front where she saw Roary's legs dangling like a 'Michelangelo' bronze as he sat on the plastic table outside. Vivid shaped, glistening wet in the torrid sunlight. Bronzed muscles of torso and thighs gracefully relaxed . . . . Face still immature but a strong clean-cut determined jaw . . . fine lips, slightly petulant, curly brown hair, wide-eyed, button-nosed and deep-chested . . . A starved woman's dream and a young woman's ambition to seduce.

She filled with desire to know him intimately.

She thought to herself how wonderful another human presence can be.

Unkindly people might judge that she was incommoded by too many red corpuscles in her richly romantic blood, or that one was over-sexed and under-satisfied by her husband.

Rodney Fletcher was next to Roary, right arm resting lightly on his shoulder as though for support. Smaller, well-knit wiry frame, with a warm sensitive expression on his face, with modest reservations, as though finding all this novelty very adventurous.

"He's a great kid isn't he? He whispered shyly into Roary's ear."

"Yes, I like his style. I wonder how his Ma is though! Looks pretty tough to me."

At that moment, Jezebel and her step-son (loved as her own, as she'd had two Caesareans with her former Italian husband) both arrived at their table. She carrying a tray with glasses and Coca Colas glistening icy from the freezer.

"Buen georno, my boys! How do you like our lovely beach?" As she placed the drinks on the table in such an expansively elegant manner. Only possible in this climate and made convincingly charming and genuine by Latins. She qualified for that distinction, being born in her father's restaurant half way along the via Alfonsine, in Naples ten years before the Second World War began.

"How's yourself too?" Roary ventured delicately, as he saw in her pleasantly coarse Neapolitan face, that she'd passed her best. She noticed him responding simply as a self-conscious youth to her unique vitality: a social aura which in his short life in the States, he had never encountered in such a gypsy style. She made him feel great.

"Bitte?" (Please?) She said enquiringly. Head cocked pretending not to catch his American drawl, which in turn gave her a surreptitious chance to give him a deep provocative glance with her black eyes smiling a challenge at him.

She liked even more what she now saw, an unawakened proud young male, trying to be furtive and into her depth but failing. He still had a dream-like quality in his boyish face. Not the cynical knowing look of drug-addicts, sexists or libertines. A face instinct with ardour and obvious innocence.

The 'Three Musketeers' sat and drank their Cokes, whilst Jezebel bawled to Eric inside: "Bring the boys some food." This rather vaguely, then more precisely, she asked, "What will it be? Hamburgers with onions, cheese and salad?"

"Yeh," agreed Roary. "Guess we could all do with one of each. Fill up with the old carbohydrates after our dip."

"Well not exactly," she corrected. "Ours are real beef and ham – take your pick, do you good." She very nearly added 'Puts lead in your pencil too,' but thought better of it.

"OK then we'll have the sandwiches, and do you have Vino Roco?" he asked, a trifle unsure of himself as she opened three more Cokes end collected plates from tourists at an adjoining table.

"Sure we have muscat, vino, ron, whisky. But you are too young aren't you?" she challenged.

"No restrictions in France, Spain and Portugal, remember." He laughed with his whole body. "Boys are men after fourteen aren't they!" He exploded.

"OK smart guy." Imitating a Yankee for his delight.

"For tonight!" he said. "Not now . . . Wanna celebrate a little now we drove right here on your oily old beach with your great kid Johan."

Johan listened carefully to this conversation and thought it a good moment to broach the idea of camping out with his two new friends from America tonight. He said casually in such a disarmingly innocent manner.

"It's OK then if I join them to sleep in their tent Jez?" He sounded grown up and independent in front of his bigger pal. "Then I can take their vino in an ice-bucket and spuds to roast on the fire embers. Vino, dead cool in ice-bucket." He emphasised. "You can join us and sing us an Italian love song too."

"Well Johan, my dear! If you promise me you won't

wander off to the dunes or along the beach alone after dark! You know how dangerous it is! Three robberies at the restaurant and one at the flat before we removed to the Villa away from the beach. Don't forget to take your sleeping-bag. You don't make yourself a nuisance with your pals from America."

"Don't you worry about him, Ma. We'll take good care of him tonight," Rod reassured her.

"Oh he's not a sissy. Don't get me wrong! He's like his father used to be. Likes adventure, same as he did once!" she said dejectedly. "Now he's only interested in making money and spending it on sexy girls. No more war to fight so he's gone soft, except for bullying poor old Harold."

"Well that's settled for tonight," Roary remarked. "Only remains to pay you for these refreshments and to order two bottles of vino which I'll pay for right now." As he stretched his torso for her to admire and his pals to know this is just what a grown-up guy does to handle this situation, he took out two fifty peseta pieces from his tiny pocket in his trunks. (His whole body shown off to its best to this challenging woman from that ancient city of Naples, who seemed to have some of the smouldering fire of Vesuvius in her veins.) At last he paid her and she gripped his right hand in both of hers as she took the money, giving him a warmth all over.

Johan felt big and important as well as possessive towards Roary. Rod admired him constantly since Roary rescued him from a beating by a gang of hoodlums outside the school-precincts two years ago. Jezebel felt secret pleasure from the boy's responsiveness to her. She excused herself and returned to the bar.

Johan said to his friends, "Wait a minute. I'll go and fetch Sugar then I'll show you the south beach big rollers!"

They were just leaving when Harold entered and bade

them a discreet, "Ha, good morning boys, catch any Mermaids whilst swimming this time?"

He tried to sound butch and nonchalant, but was almost in a shiver of delight at seeing such healthy youngsters enjoying real comradeship. So he continued to gaze at them in side glances as they strolled off together towards the dunes in the south where they could bathe completely nude, and Sugar barked her approval and raced into the sea to get a stick thrown by Rod.

Harold had seen them earlier, which had filled him full of aesthetic satisfaction, mixed with nostalgia for his own departed youth. He had seen them both disappear inside their tent to lie fully stretched to test it out for their length. He cunningly arranged his work-bench so as to just have them in view whilst he worked carving Jezebel's windmill blades. Enabling him to savour two pleasures at once. The lithe beauty of unconscious youth (which gave such epicurean delights to old admirers) coupled with this marvellous shimmering light, making his work and appreciation of male symmetry an endless and healthy source of inspiration. For, in more sombre moods, he felt that the seductive allure of females (although necessary for reproduction) was not strong enough to fortify one against the encroaching spiritual desert of western life, here on this much abused 'Island of Love'.

How could he convince others it is best to live simply, applying a few clear principles of recycling waste and harnessing resources in order to respect ecological imperatives. Do we have to have another nuclear disaster like Chernobyl in Russia before we're all convinced of the dangers of scientific negligence and criminal arrogance?"

Are we all just waiting for the end . . . not caring what we do or how we do it as we fill up our days before the final curtain on the drama of the human race?

Such were his thoughts as he saw them merge with the thousands of indifferent tourists.

And men such as he? He mused pensively. An absolute menace. For how can all the world live in tents, caravans or care and do just as they want like himself? Paying no taxes, buying no insurance: except where legally necessary. A danger to status quo morals, a damp squib on business (of the profit first kind). And if he had any say: poor people would not be exploited. Nations and Nationalities would be declared obsolete and passports burnt.

But he was a vacillating character all the same. Unashamedly . . . for isn't the world threatened at this moment by those who know what they want and attain it in an unscrupulous way, whatever the price our frail humanity pays?

Sadly, he watched youngsters building sandcastles and had anxious feelings about the environment which they were obliged to accept as 'normal' for the unfolding of their lives.

Presently he turned to Eric for consolation of his morbid thoughts.

"Hello Eric, how's everything? Nothing more from your deserted wife trying to catch up with you and sue you for neglect?"

"Not heard anything from her. Seen no private detectives hanging around either. She's not so innocent though. Maybe she's suffering from a guilty conscience more than me."

"Oh, it's all this over-refined food people are eating these days. Making them hyperactive and morally decadent. Well forget your troubles Eric. We can't change the world. It's good if we change ourselves a bit I guess."

"Well Harold, this job I have doesn't make it any easier.

All this seductive holiday talent walking into my lecherous arms every night."

"Forget it, Eric!" Harold exclaimed. "Live now pay later: as they say. Give's a packet of Gitans please, Eric?" He sat smoking and thinking.

A whimsical spontaneous friend if ever there was one. Imperfect . . . part vagabond, hard working assistant, and part a wild seducer of holidaying females who wanted a bit on the side. A mixed up young man . . . but very much alive and attractive.

"Olah Harold!" piped in Jezebel. "On the house Harold! One Pilsner Gold-label for Harold and don't charge for his cigarettes Eric."

"You're so kind Jezebel."

"It's one of those days, Harold! Business is good . . . my son has found valuable new friends from America . . . keeps one young doesn't it? He means such a lot to me these days. Not much else worth living for is there?"

Harold sensed she wanted to make up for Horst's ugly attack on him the day before so he said pleasantly, "Mind if I climb up and measure for the wind-wheel post?"

"No, not at all Harold. There's a ladder at the back."

"Thanks . . . shouldn't take long. I'll have it up tomorrow. Have you any colour preference?"

"No, leave it to you, and by the way: Here's the money Horst owes you in this envelope."

"Oh you are such a good sport, Jez. Thanks very much. All is forgiven and forgotten. Psychedelic then, with spots. Should look good. Bring late customers in! Bye-bye."

3

Drab outlines of apartment-blocks east of the beach faded into greys and indigos at night looking like sinister sentinels of doom. Harold preferred the robust but eternal movement of the ocean, so changed parking places to a copse of trees that looked west to the beach and moon-lit horizon.

"Mind if we make our camp-fire near you Harold?" Roary's voice demanded out of the gathering gloom.

"Delighted to oblige young man! Don't mind me. Just take care of the trees and grass; what there is of it . . . So dry now!"

"It's OK with Harold! Bring the faggots. Put 'em here near these trees." He shouted. As Rod and Johan panted up from the beach loaded with drift-wood.

"There y'are . . . that's enough for tonight."

"Mind if I take out the brass screws from that old chest before you burn it lads?"

"Not a bit Harold . . . help yourself! We'll burn it later or not at all . . . Bit of good mahogany that!" Observed Roary.

"We daren't make a big fire and in any case we're only baking a few potatoes, and heating a pan of soup," explained Rod.

"Thanks boys. Those screws are useful in my work and who knows, there may be something in that tiny locked draw in the corner of the old seaman's chest!

Rod came close to inspect and said, "Yeh, I guess you'll have to force it open tomorrow in the daylight. There . . . it'll be safe next to your car."

"Come on you guys! Don't sit on your bums. Help me make a fire-place with these rocks." Rod indicated with his arm.

They set to work like seasoned cow-punchers settling for the night under the star-studded sky of a Texas prairie.

"A couple of cartons, Johan! Here, catch . . . turn 'em upside down . . . make a table." This order came from Harold inside the VW.

The young German fixed them perfectly . . . face aglow with excitement.

"Do you have cutlery, plates, mugs and glasses etc, Harold?"

"Yes indeed Roary, knives, forks, just enough. I'll use an upturned pan-lid for soup and a small pickle-jar for wine. You've invited me I take it?"

"Oh yes! We like your style of life . . . being a nomad and making a living the way that you do. All those tools you carry and so much variety in your life."

"Yes but no money in it. Only enough to scrape along: hand to mouth; but as you say . . . A lot of freedom from the normal grindstone of life!"

"Not like my dad!" chipped in Johan.

"No, I guess your pop likes money, security and the usual status symbols . . . No jam-butties for him! Like my Dad in Boston USA." Roary remarked.

Johan didn't understand 'status-symbols' at eleven years old, but got the idea well enough.

"Come on . . . let's take it easy now. You look all in Johan!"

"Ja, ja. I'll come and sit with you."

He sat between Rod's legs, resting his head on the bigger boy's chest and his small bum on the warm sand. Then, looking drowsily at the soup bubbling on the fire, he relaxed completely in Rod's arms by placing his hands on Rod's thighs. A few minutes later Rod embraced the younger boy full length in the sandy hollow. He cuddled him close to give him confidence now he was so tired.

"I've a surprise for you boys!"

Harold appeared from the back of his car with a big dish of salad and more than a kilo of fresh sardines in a net bag.

"These'll go down well with baked potatoes; soup, salad and wine," said he happily. "Johan told me about the early catch. So, grilled sardines too: thanks to Johan. Hope you all like fresh fish?" he questioned.

"You ain't kidding, Harold! Just fine eating: after a big day skinny-dipping and chasing each other like wild-savages in the nude, down at the southern tip. We've run miles today. Almost too tired to eat." Rod sat up, explaining to Harold and fixing the fire with sticks.

"Well . . . why don't you fellows go for that nocturnal swim you promised yourselves before supper?"

"Brilliant Harold! The warm water'll put a bit more life into us," Roary offered.

"Here, have a glass of Muscatel before you go! Give you courage. Then you'll be raring to eat supper." He poured it out and handed it over.

"Leave the cooking to me. I'll take over Roary, whilst you keep your eye on the two younger ones . . . OK?"

"Agreed Harold," said Roary.

"Don't swim to Morocco though. Ten minutes and supper's ready."

"OK," they all chimed in harmony, as they raced off after gulping the sweet wine.

Harold sat smoking a Gitan cigarette; carefully cleaning the fish. He filled with wonder at how simply and perfectly youngsters love each other whilst free from parents, school and any form of authority, and when together under a star-lit sky.

Patter patter of wet feet and panting bodies gasping for

breath and they were back.

"Oh Johan, what's that on your feet and legs? Come to the fire. Oh it's an oil-slick ball you've trodden in. Well it had to be for one of you. Never mind, there's worse things happen at sea!"

"Hold on Harold, I've got a Jerry-can of petrol."

"Thanks Roary. Good idea. I'll get a torch as we have to clean him up away from the fire. Then wash off with soap and water. Take over kitchen duties please Roary. Try the spuds with a stick. If they give they're done," Harold commanded.

Harold cleaned Johan up in a couple of shakes whilst the two pals saw to the dinner, and watched the fire didn't get out of control when the wind veered.

"Eh Harold, a few sardines still wriggling about. How did you keep them fresh all day?" enquired Rod, who had taken over heading and tailing and laying them neatly in the wire grill.

"Well I bought them straight from the boat when they beached. Thirty pesetas . . . and over a kilo. They didn't weigh 'em. Great guys, those fishermen. Different as gold from brass, compared with that crowd of tourists living over there." He pointed with a stabbing finger of accusation to the hideous hotels and apartments out east.

"Tourists bring in the money though," remarked Roary, defensively as he stirred the fire with a steel piece off an old bed-stead found on the beach.

"Agreed Roary, but there's two sides to that you know! Not enough water for tomato and banana growers here in the south because it is syphoned off to this 'new town'. Many workers have taken hotel or restaurant jobs as cheap labour for rich entrepreneurs who've bought up the best sites on coastal areas and developed them hideously as you see here. It's their Island no longer. Much of it is already sold off to German, American, Dutch and Swedish speculators. If it goes on much longer even the fishermen will have no free beach to land their catch."

The boys listened attentively to this out-of-school piece of education, then Roary retorted, "The locals earn more money doing this work."

"Oh sure . . . but what's the use of money if you've sold your birthright and can only survive by working for foreigners? Their nature is adulterated! They're losing contact with their own soil. Boys on the streets in Las Palmas, selling their youth for cash . . . forgetting their cheerful though austere mode of 'work hard and play hard'."

Harold was quite worked up and needed physical movement so he poked the embers and flattened them ready for the grill.

"Come on then Harold. Now that's all over tell us how the hell you kept the fish fresh all day?" demanded Roary.

"Is the grub ready?" cut in Rod of Roary, who by now decided to celebrate the day and the pow-wow supper with a Red Indian nude dance. Beginning with slow removal of his bathing trunks. He looked wonderful in the dancing flames when the wind fanned the embers. He finished in fine style leaping over the fire and circling it in rhythmic jumps alternating with spreadeagled arms and legs in a 'Yoga' acceptance of all life. He sat down breathless and Harold, who had been in ecstatic delight to see such uninhibited 'Nature Worship', declared supper to be, "Just about perfect."

He placed the wind-wheel blades on top of the roof-rack to dry off, put his tools away and returned to inspect the fish sizzling away.

"Let's have salad and baked potatoes as starters, and now . . . a glass of good Spanish Muscatel. Here's to all good people and natural life everywhere. And as for keeping the sardines fresh? Well, now you're all still sober, I'll explain."

He sat on a friendly rock and balanced his plate on his knee.

"I put 'em in a mosquito netting with a stone for sinker fixed to a line. Then drop them into a deep shady cove over there." Pointing to a jagged rock formation of volcanic black, barely visible now as the night sky advanced. He continued excitedly.

"There's a real pirate's cave just behind that inlet and I shouldn't wonder if that old chest you found wasn't once inside the timbers of a pirate's ship. Water-logged, and been there ages, until you found it today."

"Eh, what do you know about that then, you guys? The old pirate's cove refrigerator."

"Ah, a very practical cold-store," observed Johan slowly and precisely. "For how could it be a refrigerator, when it could not freeze anything?" He didn't agree with Roary. It was too ambiguous for his Teutonic brain to accept. For he'd heard his dad and step-mum discussing the freezer in the Kontiki. It was electric and when the diesel folded one day before Christmas, last year, Harold came over and repaired it. No Spaniard would work during Christmas. All the food would have gone bad if it hadn't been for Harold's response to an emergency.

Which only showed how useful old dreamy hippies can be to the rich and the slick business people on this once so beautiful natural paradise. Now, alas, sadly desecrated with fourteen hideous kiosk restaurants; balls of fuel-oil tossed out by an angry ocean; a garish new holiday-town, spilling over, almost to the water's edge: swiftly built and an eyesore to those who know Venice and Florence in Italy, and the superb villages, bars and public buildings, built over decades and with unerring good taste, on the Greek Islands in the Aegean.

"Pretty awful mess they've made of the Island haven't they?" offered Harold, as he grilled the second lot of fish.

"Yes, not much style . . . just practical I guess . . . like most things these days. Young girls on the pill in order to have fun with no problems. Boys putting condoms on if they sleep with girls before getting married. The same kind of rationalisation," observed Roary thoughtfully as he cleaned his plate and held it for Harold to give him more sardines.

"Anyone for any more fish, spuds salad? Come on lads, we have to eat all this, then there's the soup."

Rod and Johan came close and replenished their plates. Rod was in love with life. He listened to the mellow ebbing sound of the ocean, looked at the lithe shape of the young German and felt a strange haunting protectiveness towards him.

"All it wants here is a few straw-covered beach-huts for travellers like us and maybe a bar or two. Get away from all this trivia and really relate to each other without stimulants, crashing 'music', or guilt-complexes, engendered by consuming whilst others starve," said Harold in emphatic tones.

"Far more fun doing it yourself under the open sky with a few friends than having it all set out and then (not being tired or hungry as we) apt to leave half on the plate as I have seen."

"Yeh Rod, you're right. Tourists want everything laid out. Nothing to do except gorge themselves silly, then see a doctor for dyspepsia later."

"Agreed! My Ma and Pa were here last year so I know the score OK."

The fire dimmed, so Harold lit his storm-lantern and hung it on a branch close by.

"This'll bring night moths and maybe a mosquito or so but we can see what we are eating. Hope there's no oil inside the fish! I hope the trawler caught them well out so they won't be contaminated."

"These look good Harold," Rod said, as he tucked in and doused his with salt and a dab of butter. "Taste super too!"

"More wine? Come let's open the second bottle. Fill up boys, give me your glasses. What's in the soup, Rod? Let me guess! He struck a pose, leaning against the tree like an ancient court-jester. "Canary Island soup a L'Rodney Fletcher, chef de cuisine. My Menu:

"Moon-beams . . . dancing star-light . . . sweet ozone, wafted in on the bosom of a gentle breeze . . . comradeship and the best of company on a dreamy beach."

"Right you are Harold. Plus onions, carrots, aubergines, peppers, spuds and a few chicken-pieces from the super-market."

"Come on then! Don't forget the Muscat. We'll eat well, drink deep and sleep soundly tonight after all this. And what about you sleepy-eyes?" enquired Roary to Johan . . . "A little wine for you too?"

"Yes, just a little with water please, as my dad said not to get drunk at coming up to twelve. He said it isn't good for me. I've had wine, beer, even whisky with Eric in the bar when my father goes to Las Palmas on his nights off. Not too much Harold, as I am sleepy already."

Suddenly pandemonium up top. A car's powerful lights stabbed the darkness away from the beach coming to rest opposite Pedro's (Peter's) white Mercedes van. Exchange of official voices. Sonorous commands breaking the peaceful night. Peter's voice was heard saying agitatedly.

"No señor . . . Nix goot . . . Nine."

Rod ran up the escarpment to get a better view. Harold felt impotent, just when he wanted to help Peter . . . who'd proved himself to be such a staunch friend when Harold was in trouble.

Sometimes life is so terribly cruel. Peter killed during the war; and now he was obeying his best impulses to spread a little joy . . . albeit not quite legal joy, yet joy all the same and he has to pay.

Poor Peter was pulled out bodily and hustled into the police-van by the Guardia Civil. His van was systematically searched. Then locked secure by the police patrol. Happily they were too engrossed to visit the small copse of trees below the car-park where they were. Almost within throwing distance from where the angry retired former SS stormtrooper had parked his white Mercedes and from which he had been unceremoniously extracted.

Later it was learnt that Peter (Pedro as he preferred) sold beer to the nudists in the south and organised handball and netball games for them. He'd made a handsome profit from both.

The police found twenty-thousand pesetas in the van. 'Pedro' was interrogated and imprisoned for three days. Then dismissed from the Island on the first boat out, never to return. His money? Confiscated, for he sold beer without a vendor's licence

Harold felt anxious too, because he worked without a permit. So when the commotion took place Harold told the boys to cool it and: "Keep quiet or they'll be over here. Luckily the ocean mist has swirled in." He whispered. "And these few embers aren't making any visible smoke. Better douse the lantern, in any case it'll resemble the fishermen's lights. That's why they're not coming over here to investigate."

They all sat near the almost dead fire pondering the day's adventure, and Harold poured the coffee.

"Well boys we can relax now. They've gone. I'll go round to see Peter tomorrow and try to cheer him up. I hope your stomachs are just about to burst and that you've had enough excitement for one day?"

"I'm very tired and it has been a great day but please Harold just one question before we part. Is there nowhere on earth where people can be really free?"

"Rod, my dear friend, it is a big question but in brief as you have seen with Peter a few minutes ago, there is never any unqualified freedom without responsibility towards each other and to all the free beautiful places in nature itself.

"We have the responsibility to guard that beauty that we see in each other and in all life where it is still untouched by man. In fact, I'll tell you all my secret, I hope before I die to set up a small place of peace. A lovely corner to which anyone may come and feel refreshed. And I hope my boys you will remember this day and your love for each other as a talisman of what can be achieved when we live for each other and the God that made All rather than to feather our own nests at the expense of others."

"Question answered, Harold! Many thanks. I wish my pop said things that you do. What do you say Roary?"

"I'm not gonna say anything. I'm just full up with feelings of love for the whole world right now, after what he's just said 'cause it's so true. We just have to protect each other and the quiet lovely wild places that remain."

"Oh look . . . Johan is asleep already. Rod, can you manage him or do you need help to carry him to the tent?"

"No thanks. Good-night Harold. I'll give him the old fire-man's lift. See you tomorrow, Harold! Thanks for a real

f

banquet supper. Cheers."

"Happy dreams lads! Sleep close."

They were soon cuddled up close in a protective cluster of budding vitality and dropped off into the dreams of happy youngsters everywhere.

Next day Harold breakfasted as usual and then decided to remove all the screws from the chest and force open the draw as the lock was rusty. At last the screws were safe in his tool box and the old seaman's chest fell apart. A small bundle dropped to the hard baked sand. He removed the canvas cover which disintegrated at a touch. A small leather purse almost rotten with age, seemed heavy for its size. At last the treasure!

Twenty gold sovereigns, dated? Well he couldn't make them all out because of discolouration. He rubbed them in the sand then polished them with vim and water and found they were all marked early eighteen hundreds.

He made a big pot of coffee.

"Come on lads, breakfast is ready," he shouted across to the green tent, pegged about ten metres distant.

The sleepy heads popped through the tent flap.

"Morning Harold," Roary offered. "You're up early ain't you?"

"Yes. We've got to clean up this campfire place and coffee's ready."

They duly arrived. Big grins of pleasure on their faces at the prospects of another day's adventuring together.

Harold poured, and then, whilst in a circle taking breakfast he threw his grass mat in the middle then placed the heap of sovereigns onto it. A happy though inquisitive look in his old eyes.

"What shall we do with these, my hearties? They're yours by rights. So it's up to you three. They are old coins which are quite valuable now."

"Oh boy, what a mercy you are an ecologist Harold. We'd have put that old chest on the fire if it hadn't been for you wanting to save the bronze screws!" exclaimed Rod.

"Yes and the wind would have soon blown sand over the ashes and the money would have gone for ever," Roary observed excitedly."

"Nature loves those who love Her," Harold said.

Then there was the silence of suspended animation. No one knew what to say or do. Perhaps all too shy to say. Harold ventured, "What if we give ten sovereigns to famine relief . . . Save the Children Fund . . . Oxfam. Ten at three hundred dollars an ounce in pure gold comes to quite a handsome donation to a good cause. The rest we divide equally. Two and a half each in cash. How about that?"

"Yes, sure." They all chorused heartily.

Two months later, Roary Westland and Rodney Fletcher were in High School, puzzling over comparative religions, quadratic equations and French irregular verbs. Johan had graduated to the senior section of his school. Harold found work in another restaurant for a kindly boss. They had all tasted a unique island soup . . . not on everyone's menu; and the two pals from the States felt more mature for their first trip abroad. Meeting up, in such unexpected ways with a mixture of the sordid, the poetic, the beautiful, the living and the dead in the European Heritage.

They both agreed:

"Stodgy 'OLD UNCLE SAM', wasn't such a bad old guy after all."

6

The Meeting
(A true friend shelters like a tree)

Down in a rugged department named Herault in Languedoc, Southern France, Andrew Sheldon from England began building a wooden cabin. November, in nineteen seventy-five, was mild with many sunny days and warm sultry nights inviting him to work until late with shirt off and shorts on. Near completion in late February of seventy-six, he wore warm sweaters, two pairs of trousers and socks, to keep his old bones efficient for working in the cold brisk air sweeping the valley from the peaks of the snow-capped Pyrenees, some forty Kilometres away to the south-east.

As days lengthened, Dolly's doggy coat of russet on her body, black ears, with a pure white flash on her breast, glistened with good health. Her big butch honey-coloured son, Rasputin, accompanied her foragings into the rocky scrub nearby and the thick forests in the fertile valley of the river Brian, as it raced with melting snow some thousand feet below and a mile distant from the cabin.

Both awakened earlier than usual to go off to the delights of the chase. Returning an hour later with a half-consumed rabbit or a disgusting piece of dead goat or sheep carcass, victims of their sharp teeth or the cold winter, the latter mellowing as the days lengthened and cherry orchards showed swellings of leaf-buds.

Even so, both dogs curled up inside Andrew's small tent as the mist descended and evening dictated a warm meal and a good sleep. Dreaming! so necessary for all three to refresh and renew energies for game still to be caught and the south side of the cabin to be nailed on with an old Arabic hand-made hammer, a souvenir from Jeddah, bought in an Arab souk ten years ago.

The roof was on and he'd made the north wall of local stone; built close to the sheer rock face rearing up for a hundred feet before sloping backwards to a farm-track, running round the hill to a vineyard and beyond to the river Brian, which all three took, together with Suzie the goat, for washing, swimming and recreation in the summer months and to collect fire-wood and seasonal mushrooms near the river. Too cold now, but wait a couple of months and the barking of the dogs would waken sleepy foxes to be more vigilant about their young and startle frogs and rabbits, and make snakes curl up a little tighter in their warm nests deep below the rocky out-crops of fragile marble near the river. Badgers and wild boars gave the cabin a wide berth at all times.

Soon the chimney was finished, built from small stones set into cement mortar round an old hospital portable toilet, which he'd cut and adapted, as it was just right to make a smooth inner surface to the chimney-stack. By this means he took it as high as possible then finished with a steel tube of one and a half yards giving it a jaunty appearance. Andrew loved textural contrasts such as this. His idea of domestic sculpture. It seemed he needed to express his ideas with the minimum of fuss, the greatest economy and the best practical results. He fixed a control-rod to the trap inside, so that the fire could be regulated with just enough draught to cause good combustion without wasting precious fuel, dead wood faggots becoming scarce these days.

That was last week and now he stripped bark off the last piece of pine, trimmed it to shape and banged it on to the frame with a look of triumph. Tonight he and the dogs could dine in comfort before a cosy fire. Suzie the goat slept inside the old cave with plenty of straw bedding. He locked her in and retired.

Hopes of coming to terms with a technical Europe had waned since teaching English in Saudi Arabia. The rag-bag debris of fifty-five years of life's experiences, within technical structures, had coalesced into a dream-wish, a vague longing, a dim outline of paradise on earth. Heaven in the sky! An insubstantial fancy in most religions, had to be made concrete before he died. No wishy washy symbolic metaphors for Andrew, who often spurned those who believed in an after-life. Heaven or hell is what we make for ourselves here and now. God is present in everything and in every moment of waking life, with all it implies in terms of love, energy, passion, beauty and the pathos involved in pursuing all four, or God didn't exist at all. Perhaps heaven existed, perhaps not. No one had ever returned except in the mythical return of Jesus to his disciples, and he didn't believe in ghosts anyway. In any case, "Is there such a phenomena as an isolated soul?" he asked. "An entity completely alone, entirely isolated?" He thought not! "We are part of everything our eyes set upon, or our fingers touch, or our ears hear or our mouths taste. If we do ugly things, if we build ugly houses, streets and cities, if we listen to horrible defeatist music and indulge in sordid politics, rather than the politics of experience, then that's how we are. Like a medallion round one's neck carving one's destiny out of the wrong materials, the thick dirty mud of organised religion, or political dogma, instead finding a set of beliefs from one's own experiences."

A hard steel streak began to assert itself inside his being, inside his bones and blood. From now on he was on his own, at least physically. He knew he was surrounded with a natural beauty that couldn't be beaten but might be equalled elsewhere. And now this beauty was a pulsating ally. The very earth seemed to help his old bones in his feet walk with more spring than he'd known in his hectic miss-spent days of wondering, searching: and failing to find inner peace. Would he find it now? He didn't know for sure but his wide nostrils quivered with expectancy. Like his dogs' before setting off into the down wind, bringing delicious scents of the chase.

Only cowards want certainty! Adventure is all a man needs, besides the wherewithal to stay alive, that is. And now he'd set himself to provide just that. To make a base that supports an adventurous life. No dole queues, no stinking cities snarled up with cars, no eating of food grown by farmers who think more about profits than respect for the earth and people's stomachs. He'd make his own paradise or die. Put faith to the test to see if it was a benevolent planet or just a fortuitous nightmare.

Memories of his early ecology experiments flooded his hot dry head as he eased from planing the big oak door-frame on a late August morning the same year he'd finished his home. This was a repair job he'd contracted to do with his French friends in exchange for the piece of land he worked. Watched with the unfathomable wisdom of Dolly and Rasputin, who were both curled up together under a lovely old stone archway from the narrow drive which led to the the courtyard of the old farm-house. Over the arch ran a ramp for easy off-loading of hay, corn, straw etc, into the large granary next to where Andrew worked. It was now in a state of decrepitude, except for the ground floor, now lived in by a young French couple.

The riviera painted its patient strokes onto Andrew's body. Andrew, if nothing else, was a sensuous animal, loving a good tan before discretion. So, if a police-patrol arrived, he quickly donned light shorts over his briefs. He spied the approach road well in advance of a sudden visit.

He'd made the joints ready for gluing so re-filled the dogs' water-bowl and decided to let the chickens out for the afternoon. On returning he saw a sturdy young chap approaching: either German or Dutch, he thought, blue eyed, flaxen haired, looking clean and trim with a large green back-pack. He decided to stay in his briefs and to roll a cigarette before addressing the newcomer.

"Hi, how do? Come far then?" He offered, edging into the shady archway, after placing his jack-plane carefully, almost reverently, on its side and nervously brushing the shavings off the newly worked wood. The newcomer hesitated, shook Andrew's outstretched sweaty palm eagerly enough to show warmth, then replied with clipped exact tones with a Dutch accent.

"Yes, I walked over the Pyrenees with another French traveller and my little dog Pino."

"Oh, very good to see you. My name is Andrew, Andy for short. You look marvellously fit. Where is your dog then?"

"He's here in the front pocket of my anorak, nice and comfortable. He dipped in and took out the tiny white and biscuit coloured pup and placed her gently on the grass just under the arch. Dolly fussed her as it placed a right paw onto her nose. Rasputin looked on lazily indifferent. Not big enough yet, his doggy verdict.

"She was the only one alive of an abandoned litter left inside a carton on the road-side as I left Pamplona, before I set out on my trek along the old Pilgrim route to Compostela. Then I decided to descend through the St Bernard's pass to here."

"You must be quite tired by now. It's quite a distance."

"Yes, over two hundred miles by foot. I could do with a rest," he said in a quiet matter of fact voice. Modest, yet insistent, so different to the effusive insincerity of French nuance which was, as Andrew admitted to himself, sometimes useful in choosing to be politely obscure, rather than truthful.

Andy asked, "What's your name then?"

"I'm sorry, I forgot to introduce myself. I'm Dirk Van Gilder from Amsterdam."

A chance meeting this! Just a normal happening, one might think. An everyday affair, given modern transport, so many hippies, weirdies, campers came this way every summer. But with him Andrew set a'wondering: He's got nerve, that's for sure, going all that distance on foot. He's a compassionate chap too, especially for dogs. He's tall, good looking and youngish. Well set up in a canny individualistic way. What's his breaking point I wonder? What is it that drives him? What's he discovered about himself and life that I haven't? And I'm old enough to be his father. Well, perhaps I'll never know, but he looks a bit uncertain of himself . . . a bit lost . . . or trying manfully to find his own talisman. Maybe we are important to each other.

A silent soliloquy computed in seconds, he continued . . . "My full name is Andrew Sheldon from England. I've built a log cabin at the bottom of the valley over there." He pointed in a south-easterly direction. "If you'd do me the honour, why not have supper together inside it . . . that is if you are free and have no urgent plans?"

"Thank you very much. I'd like that! I have to ask for permission to erect my tent on the pasture over there, from the lady or gentleman at the farm. Once that's fixed I'll be free to join you."

Like a magnetic charge drawing them together . . . as though thirsting to drink from the well of each other's experiences and draw from each other the mysterious qualities of each other's maleness. One having what the other needed. Different wine matured at disparate times and pressed from vineyards of life both geographically and climatically foreign, coming together to form a heady cocktail.

"Come then, let me introduce you and Pino your lady dog to M'lle Angèle Lacost, the natural wife of Mr Andre Ducasse?"

"Yes, but first I'll let Pino play with your dogs on the grass and drink fresh water. She's nervous, had an accident inside the tent: boiling water, some fell onto her head and a small patch of hair came off. She's OK but I'll give her some time to make friends with your dogs."

"A sound plan indeed. Dolly will teach her a few tricks. She's only twenty months old . . . ten months with me . . . and Rasputin her son from her first litter, he is only nine months but nearly fully grown as you can see. Dolly is a very fertile lady, unhampered by niceties of human sexual ethics or feelings of fidelity to one husband. I believe she thinks that there are far too many humans and it is necessary for her to redress the balance. She's already pregnant again."

Andrew wondered at that moment: What are the sex instincts of Dirk? What are his social views? Did he believe in a historical interpretation of life? or a religious one? or was he clever enough to combine both in a passionate committal to nature? or was he like himself, making his own religion from direct experience of all these strands as he evolved each day? All unanswered . . . a veritable unworked human mine, an Aladdin's cave to be explored delicately by both. He hoped fervently that today would set the pattern. Andrew started mining into the subliminal depths of another soul in such a disarmingly shrewd manner thus . . .

"What started you off on this Pyrenees trip Dirk, may I ask?"

"Well, I had asthma badly and my doctor advised me to leave Amsterdam . . . even forsake my job as a plastics mould designer in my father's factory. He said I was suffering from emotional trouble and too much sterilised food intake. He said for me to eat fresh fruits and vegetables and wholemeal bread and go for long walks in the country-side and forget work for as long as possible."

"So you looked at the maps and decided upon the Pyrenees range. Quite an adventurous choice, eh?"

"Yes, rather, for I hadn't done any long distance tramping. As you know, Holland is flat and damp in winter, quite unsuitable for walking but OK for biking."

"Yes, a bit like England I suppose. Your doctor seems to be a social thinker . . . an environmentalist. He sent you to the trees, hills, flowers and rivers, rather than to a psychoanalyst or a priest of religion, in order to cure you of asthma?"

"Homeopathic doctors consider the person in the whole of his/her environment. He diagnosed my trouble as emotional and psychological, you see my father and mother are divorced and when this happened four years ago I became quite sick . . . worried! But now you see, I'm quite fit again."

"Yes, you certainly look A1 now. Let's go into the farm-house with the dogs. Angèle is the lady of the house and we'll drink a glass of rouge to celebrate your arrival."

"OK, let's do that, I'm glad to meet your friends."

Andrew enthused about out-door living, stroking the dogs who jumped and barked their approval, as they walked towards the friendly looking cluster of grey stone-walled two-storey-high buildings, the centre one, being the largest, opened from a small court-yard facing south. Geraniums in a tub to the left gave a crimson splash and phlox, petunias, roses and fox-gloves, vied with each other in the centre garden, all seeming to prosper from the shade of an elegant tree on the right. Small green figs forming beneath exotic leaves giving grace, stature to the court-yard and definitive shade to the rich bed of colourful flowers in the centre. Andrew would be there picking them in late autumn, when big black and juicy, just before they fell. Angèle's dog Titus, signalled their approach with an unfriendly growl, but with tail dancing, it was obviously a doggy ploy, keeping her end up and yet giving a reluctant welcome to the visitors.

Would he turn out to be yet another coldly calculating young man or would he become a staunch ally? Perhaps not a soul-mate but at least a good reliable pal in a maddeningly disintegrating world? Didn't he really need a friend just now! Alone with no easy French linguistic skills. Often misunderstood and didn't he misjudge events, people and even the customs of the French? Anyway, he felt a surge of unusual confidence with Dirk beside him. Why should he doubt himself? The old door had been left to rot over the years just for him to come along, in God's appointed time, in order to repair it. The same went for the cars he'd repaired . . . could all this be just chance? He needed emotional . . . even sexual confidence though, something that no amount of technical competence could provide.

Many others seemed to have this way with women, without proving themselves in the work-a-day-world of work. Was he missing out or was God saving him from romantic shipwreck, which was common these days? They'd not looked too deeply into each other's eyes yet but that will come . . . flash points . . . moments of soul searching.

Andrew at fifty-nine, remembered how confused were his own ideas at thirty. Yes, he ruminated as they pushed open the kitchen door, how he'd become an existentialist in the French tradition. An irreligious idea developed and purveyed by Albert Camus and Jean Paul Satre in the fifties, but probably espoused in the first instance by Rene Descartes the mathematical philosopher, who coined the phrase.

'I think hence I exist.' Like them, he'd discarded custodian morality as being a hotchpotch with as little connection to real moral conduct, as a ship's anchor has to that of the engine turning the propellers. So, long ago, he'd pulled up the anchor.

"Hello Angèle, here's Dirk from Holland, via the Pyrenees." She dripped her head from the plastic basin resting on the marble sink let into the thick wall near the metre square window, letting in the afternoon sun which made her hair reflect silver with gold tints as she rinsed off the shampoo, and whilst rubbing her long tresses vigorously, turned towards her guests in a slightly embarrassed manner. Quickly recovering and ignoring their rude entry into her house, she wrapped a towel round like an Arab Sheik's wife and offered her shiny cheeks to them both in turn . . . the usual ritual in every French home. So pleasant an introduction, marking them off as an extremely civilised people, compared with the English for example, who are trained to suppress, or even worse, despise any show of feeling unless for winning the pools, securing lucrative contracts and attacking the opposing team supporters, if the home-team loses.

Angèle, being an expert at public relations, decided that boredom was her one deadly enemy, the one constant evil that afflicted her more than any other, so for the last few years she'd accepted a weird assortment of flotsam and jetsam into her wide old kitchen with its very old two and a half metre mahogany table, two benches unbacked, a wide fireplace, rather ugly and dusty now but a roaring pine-smelling comfort in the winter months. Little else adorned except a few nondescript trinkets on the mantle-piece and a rather elegant grandfather clock far left, near an old cupboard let into the wall. The clock had not measured out the fortunes, good or bad for those living for the last six years here, but gave a symbolic ornamentation to the stark interior, for time stops here, and to prove it, cobwebs hung delicately from wall to clock and from clock to wall.

All seemed to shock Dirk with his Dutch obsession for hyper-cleanliness, although he gave little away, except his kiss was, to the observant eye, a timid peck of formality, showing reserve, reticence, and controlled passion, so common in those from northern climes.

"True to form!" thought Andy, "breeding and class show, in people as well as horses, dogs and camels but doesn't such restraint destroy spontaneity and in so doing cuts out much that is admirable?"

Angèle, being an iconoclast, ever since reading about the emancipation of women by Simoné de Boufort, scrambled into a loose cotton petticoat over her bare body to please no one except herself. It was wide with a gathered-in effect at the waist, a border of pink roses at the bottom hem. Her bottom half discreetly covered but natural from navel up. She promptly poured rouge, filling two glasses and a pewter tumbler to their brims with a very steady hand, holding the heavy wicker-covered wine-jar. She raised her tumbler distinguishing her in a uniquely rustic manner. Her big blue-grey eyes and well-shaped head, forming a symphony of physical movement, startlingly elegant, defiant and warmly human all at once. Here was, in physical form, a living saga of willfulness, an ego-trip that never halted for a single moment. At fifty-nine she looked remarkably well preserved, not any flab on her spare wiry body, even wrinkles were few and added dignity rather than advertising her age in her worldly-wise face. She caressed the dogs, all three and fussed over Pino, putting the pup on the table to choose a few scraps left from a late lunch which still adorned the untidy table. First things first with M'lle Angèle. "Bon sante a tous," she said in a strong voice of good timbre, not gentle or delicate but a voice full of character, ordinated by an agile mind behind her larynx.

Dirk took off his anorak revealing a light blue shirt beneath. His back-pack he left outside in the courtyard, a delicate gesture of respect. Andrew responded in English. "Here's to us and any more as free as us!" he flourished a bare arm with chest proudly stuck out and legs comfortably draped from the big Spanish style chair on the right, he rubbed his middle with relish as the good wine found a congenial throat and receptive stomach.

Angèle guided the pup away from the uncovered butter, for her nose was already performing its evolutionary purposes, she said, "Please help yourself to wine," as she moved quickly to the window south and pushed a young cockerel from his audacious perch on the windowsill and turned enthusiastically to her guests.

"Well Dirk, how's things with you on this hot afternoon?"

"A little tired but OK, glad to be here in your house."

"Here, have a piece of goat's cheese and a chunk of home-made bread. Andrew is our boulanger (baker). The currant-bread has all gone, but this will do you good," said she, as she cut and served expansively, if a little self-indulgently.

Arrangements agreed; for Dirk to sojourn on a pleasant pasture below the house and near the fountain with water-trough for bathing.

"Don't leave your tent open or the goats will eat your food," she finally remarked, then turned to the flour-mill and began to grind fresh looking whole wheat ready for the next baking.

Both men paid their respects and Andrew continued gluing and clamping the new pieces onto the bottom of the oak-door panels until six pm. Dirk being a willing audience and the dogs lazily curled beneath the cool archway, sensing that human as well as doggy harmony, had entered in.

"Quite an interesting place, isn't it?" Dirk said.

"You can say that again and again Dirk, never bored here, a continuous drama, M'lle Angèle disregards all conventions that might cramp her style, in favour of grass-roots contact, she's a kind of perpetual media, using herself as a composite of television, radio, and magazine rolled into one. Her favourite quality is spontaneity and she isn't too particular who she's being immediate with. Obviously in moments of crisis, an excellent quality . . . basic to survival, but not with everyone at all times. So often times she's involved in small domestic concerns, which consume all her time and energy and so 'lord of misrule' or 'queen of chaos' takes over, but as you say, it is quite a place, for it is never static. Some would say it is actively a disorderly house. Having known them both for two years I admire what they try to do, although not always agreeing with their scale of priorities."

"How did you stumble upon such a free but rather untidy place?"

"I met a young man in a campsite at Barcelona, a Dutch man on his way to Morocco, name of Gerrard."

"Yes, he is my brother. He told me about you when he returned from his trip to North Africa."

Andrew looked up, with a look of comical confusion, from tightening the clamps on his gluing job.

"Well I'll be buggered!" he exploded . . . "Gerrard your kid brother . . . family resemblance, you've been holding out on me all this time?"

"Yes, I thought to give you a surprise."

"Quite a pleasant one, Dirk . . . great kid that brother of yours. You knew you'd meet me here then?"

"Oh yes," he said mysteriously not revealing much of his secret mind.

"Well prudence is OK with me, it makes me feel like confiding in you with impunity. There are certain differences to common problems here that seem unsurmountable. It would be interesting to have an uncommitted view, a judicious umpiring of what has happened and what might transpire in future."

"I hope I can help. What's your problem?"

"I'm trying a few experiments to live entirely on my ideas of how to apply ecology. I'll be showing you what I have done so far. I'll just finish gluing whilst you put your tent up, then we'll take a walk down for supper, OK?"

"Right, I'll see you in about ten minutes."

He mixed more Araldite, took the clamps off the door

already finished, ran the glue over the joints, let them in and clamped up. He covered over with plastic, hid his tools inside the chicken-coup, then played with the dogs, throwing a dead branch down the grassy bank. Dolly let Rasputin get it then she took it with a grip of iron and hung on till he gave up.

"That's life, the female always wins in the end!" he said moodily to himself. Where does play end and reality begin? Is it all determined by brute force as in the realistic play of animals, or do we as humans introduce subtle shades and nuances?

The two dogs relaxed and followed Andrew down to the pasture where Dirk was pushing in the last tent peg.

They both fell into step towards the fountain, filled two bidons with fresh spring water, and Andrew slipped his trunks off and lay full length in the large smoothly surfaced cement basin below it.

"Have a cool dip Dirk, no one around now, come on enjoy yourself. Give you a good appetite."

"Thanks, I will when you get out."

"Oh come on, plenty of room for the two of us."

He stripped off revealing a strong handsome body, lightly tanned all over, so Andrew guessed he was like himself, a nature boy, unashamed of his own nakedness, as though he'd gained or, in his case, perhaps never lost, his boyish innocence.

Dressed and glowingly refreshed, they took off with the dogs across the meadow towards the cabin.

"So this is your water reservoir, and that's your wind-charger above?"

"Hold on, I'll explain all when I unloose Suzie, she's been on the rope all day and wants a drink. Yes, the dam is rather crude and small but it's a start, I need every drop of water in this dry climate, in order to irrigate my garden."

"No good for bathing though?"

"No, it gets stagnant in the summer months but spring time is OK as there is plenty of melting snow flowing, but quite sharpish though like the basin up at the fountain, but not so pure."

"Why's that?"

"Because the farmer puts artificials onto his crops and I get chemicals seeping through into the dam from this terrain we've just crossed. Watch out, here comes Suzie! She goes crazy when released. She'll have you in the pond if you don't take care."

"Is she your goat?"

"Yes, she's only four months but as frisky as a naughty child. She goes for what she wants in this life and good luck to her, except when she fancies my early cabbages, carrots, lettuces, etc, even then I'm sorry I have to suppress her."

He grabbed the rope again and they strode past the wind-charger turning freely in the evening breeze from the west.

"Quite a sturdy machine and the tower built from local wood except for the platform?"

"Yes quite rustic! I make what I want from bits and pieces mainly because I have no regular income and I like the challenge of solving problems in the simplest way."

"What on earth is that?" Dirk pointed to a machine resting on the bed of the stream beyond the dam.

"It's a water-turbine. The belt turns this alternator, then the current charges the battery after passing through a rectifier. Come, I'll show you the gardens before we take supper. Hold on a moment, I'll put Suzie on her rope near to her shed then she won't feel lonely."

"Yes I notice she plays with the dogs and follows you

affectionately, except when she stops to pinch your vegetables."

"Bit of a thieving epicurean quadruped. She's determined to secure her pleasures in this life. A great philosopher, she teaches me such a lot, but my style of gardening organically won't let me indulge her appetite, except for plants that have gone to seed."

"So. . . This is it eh, 'La maison du dialogue'. Why that?"

"Long story really but it reached me because so many were interested to know why I live like a hermit down here, and during my explanations other questions crop up, so I found my cabin becoming a place where people usually feel free and glad to chew the cud a bit."

"I couldn't think of a more peaceful spot but don't you get lonely, wish for company, kids, a wife to darn your socks, etc?"

"No thank you! Teacher for twelve years. Forgive me but I am ambivalent sexually. I have to tell you this honestly before I go any further. This is partly the reason I am here doing ecology, I can't stand the competitive arena of the city where men and women vie with each other as to which shall dominate or completely possess the other. There's so much sexist bullshit around in the 'modern' world of the city, but more anon, I'll explain in more detail why I believe that we have to return to nature and respect all ecosystems in order to restore truth between men and women once more."

"You have a lovely place. I remember seeing the snow-capped Pyrenees from your path above the colline there. The cabin is sheltered, dry and snug in winter too. Your only severe problem I imagine, is water supply in a dry summer?"

"Right, except for falling rock from that rather unstable amphitheatre of nature's own making at the back, then there are composting problems, I have only one goat to make muck, so gather rotting leaves in winter months and dredge the brook out regularly, otherwise, yes I agree, very pleasant spot facing south, and after terracing as you see, the soil is no longer in danger of eroding. I hope in time to restore full tilth and continuous fertility to this very odd piece of marginal land."

"Every place has its virtues and vices I suppose. Nothing perfect on this earth. Some people like me, would say it is too spartan . . . not enough modern conveniences. No telephone, no bathroom, no toilet, no piped drinking-water, no refrigerator or television-set or washing-machine."

"Yes quite, but none of the things you mentioned are essential to life, I believe modern people are intoxicated with the pursuit; achievement acquisition and servicing of the inessential to the death of their human and distinctly humane qualities."

"Your remarks make me a fellow-traveller with profligate ego-trippers and James Bond types, who wish to remain macho enough to protect and fight for the status quo."

"Please! I didn't mean that Dirk. It's your reaction. Let's prepare supper! Tomatoes out of the greenhouse and take a cucumber please. I'll get some parsley, thyme, mint, carrots, etc. Spuds in the bake-house oven, so we can eat soon."

Andy disappeared inside preparing food, whilst Dirk surveyed the landscape in all directions. As the sun dipped he blended with the background . . . becoming part of it . . . soaking in this new feeling of himself. Richer in spirit, not because of the talk or the prospect of his first hot food for days but deeper inside. A secret part of himself emerging into a new dimension of life. No longer the monotonous stereo landscape past his bedroom-window in his native town of Amsterdam, but ever-changing textures, stark contrasts of soft delicate cloud formations with harsh unyielding rocky features, superb harmonies of trees and undulating pasture, and just now, the blending of his complete self with all the tumult and majesty of a dying day, never ever to be quite the same again. The very earth consoled his troubled mind and delicately renewed internal energies, as though putting together jagged pieces of himself, long estranged.

He looked at his hiker's legs, strong and brown, thrusting from his blue shorts, and calmly mounted the wooden steps into Andrew's home in a thoroughly composed spirit, ready to know more of Andy's ambitions and to help direct his own, over a good meal and local wine. They munched contentedly, drank deep. Andy rolled a fag.

"Your garden produce tasted really good, a fine meal, but I noticed a few grubs in the carrots and caterpillars on the cabbage."

"Yes, grubs don't matter where there's only a few. I don't use insecticides of any sort. As the soil improves, I hope to plant and sow in greater diversity, not keeping to linear sowings. This method confuses insects and gives cover for friendly birds, lizards, salamanders, frogs, moles, snakes, bees, spiders, to hide and eat up most of the aphids, black fly, grubs etc."

Andrew fed the dogs, lay back on his old divan and puffed happily, if a little nervously, at his cigarette, as Dirk stretched out on the bench near the empty fireplace and threw a few questions.

"What's your talisman in life . . . I mean your supreme moment of truth about your own life?"

"Supposing I said, the eyes of young children, birds, animals, the opening of the first buds on the trees in spring, the haunting beauty one can see in each other, that is when

142

we don't rationalise and take everyone for granted. Would that be too general? I don't like to limit the scope of truth about one's life in precise language . . . it's more than words can say!"

"Agreed, there's too many smart arses trying all the time to tie things up in nice tidy packets to be undone and consumed with a wooden fork. The feast of life I agree is not so simple as that. But in so far as you have defined your life down here in your tiny paradise, what gives you confidence to continue with very little local support, almost no money and not many visitors in the winter months?"

"Nice of you to sympathise in this way. I suppose I'm trying to prove certain ideas are correct but ideas are so mixed up with beliefs in my case, I find it difficult to slice pieces off life like cutting rounds off a French sausage. The industrialised mind likes to do this but I like the whole mess of life rather than sterilised bits seen in clinical isolation. The expert mind has brought us almost to disaster and is bringing the planet close to its death. I cannot see civilisation, as we know it, lasting more than a decade. It has to adapt to the realities of a finite resource world, or we as a species are finished."

"Does that mean leave it all to amateurs like you? Turn your back on literature, science, philosophy . . . the arts even?"

"No, I hope not! Rather a redirection, a new constellation of human endeavours, not limited to old formats or custodian fixations. Get back to nature first, then there's a chance . . . just a chance that we'll get our science, our religion, our social structures our sexual and personal problems put into perspective rather than myopic specialist traps. We have to try to see holistic life as being inter-related in dynamic ways and never static."

"Quite a programme you've set yourself. You must be a born optimist. How can we bring about such a sweeping reformation, involving as it does, a reappraisal of scientists and their research programmes? of ministers and their efforts to sooth and comfort the distressed in our automated culture? of the schools the schooled and the educators? who are presently doing their best to marry the child or student to an already threatened planet, proposing as they do, that children be proficient in adding to the GNP (gross national product) when we know that a world resource conservation strategy is imperative, if we are to avoid a cold economic war bursting into atomic genocide? In a word, most of our institutions and government agencies are adopting expedients of pragmatism without the careful use of accumulated wisdom, which we call principle."

"Have some strawberries and cream, and another glass Dirk. You've certainly underscored the real situation and the dilemmas facing each one of us. As you see I've tried to resolve a few of these personal difficulties by returning to nature in this simple way but I cannot pretend that all is well. I've had some pretty tough opposition to my efforts from the locals and one arson attempt to burn me out. But no proof, so it could just have been an accident. But even at the level of human contact things are difficult. When children come down here to visit me, I love them to feel free and do just what they want to do, except hurt or damage anything, or each other. But then, I have to take on local prejudice and narrow-minded attitudes towards foreigners."

"Then why? Why take extra problems on at your age, nearly sixty, when you could be comfortably settled in a tidy flat in England?"

Suddenly Suzie burst in from the balcony, her snapped tattered rope dangling from her collar, saluting both with a plaintive m..e..e..e..r. (Andrew sprung off his couch, caressed her and guided her nose into the left-overs from Dolly's meal. Rasputin had scoffed all his.)

"See what I mean Dirk? Real life doesn't come wrapped up, what with animals, people like Angèle and Andre, visitors like you, its always changing like the sky being dramatic. We go deep here in all our relations, so the real answer is with you. How did you feel in Amsterdam? how do you feel here? It's a question of the lap of ease and luxury, or the lap of nature for you perhaps? Feel first and reason afterwards, then decide.

"Personally I know why I am living here and doing what I do. I can't explain in words alone, language isn't enough. It's blood and bone passion too, a reaffirmation of the life-force . . . what I have left, that is!"

Andrew thought to himself, here is a vital young man in his prime, querying an old bachelor to answer the conundrum of mortal life. And what qualifications have I to answer? Me having drunk hundreds of gallons of tea, wine, beer, smoked ten kilometres of cigarettes, masturbated in love fantasies many times, thought more about my belly than ever about God and not paid any tax. Who am I to give him the answer, me a typical product of a decadent, technically industrialised, country.

They both pampered Suzie and led her to the garden, taking off her rope and installing her for the night. Andy then watered tomatoes and flowers in the gloom, then shoved the stick into the nozzle, watched by Dirk.

"You have no jet control on your hose Andy?" (Andrew returned to the real world, Dirk accepted him whatever his past or present faults.)

"No, too expensive! A piece of sharpened oak is OK, simple and effective, not much pressure . . . precious little

g

left . . . very serious in a few weeks if this heat stays."

Dirk winced an intellectual wince, thinking to himself, in the lovely beginning of the moonlit sky, what a muddle. Why didn't he make sure of the water-supply, wind-directions, a place to buy good quality timber, before building his home and gardens? Discreetly though, he followed Andrew into the darkening interior of the cabin whilst making a mental summary of the whole enterprise.

"I'm still curious . . . what makes you take risks on this piece when you could find better in England?"

"Take a seat Dirk! Coffee or tea to finish off the evening?"

"English tea please. Now come on spill the beans Andy."

"So many times you ask the same question, and I have to give ever more cunning answers. Please switch on the light Dirk. The tiny switch is above you. Thanks, that's better, I can pour tea. As to your question: After my teaching experiences in England, Saudi Arabia and a little in Spain and France and then being a hobo for some years, I decided that if you want Heaven you have to make it a daily reality in work and pray for guidance."

"No such thing as everlasting life when you die?"

"No, but if there is such a condition, then I hope it doesn't apply to me, for I can't imagine living for ever. The concept is quite beyond me. So not being enamoured of it, I prefer to do what I can see needs doing now on this marvellous planet. In any case I've already written my epitaph."

"How does it go?"

"Worms can have me when I die; Birds eat worms so thus I'll fly."

"Ha, I see you are a joker of an Englishman."

"I try not to take things too seriously, but at bottom I think it is quite serious how we live. Some religious people honestly believe this planet is a kind of mirage, merely a testing place before being admitted or excluded from everlasting life. I find this quite shocking and an insult to the one or the mystery that has made each of us. This planet is stupendously beautiful. I can't imagine paradise or a fictitious heaven above to be more sublime than what we see every day on this earth, if our eyes, ears and hearts are open, so I try to enjoy paradise on earth before the worms have a good feed. My little place has helped me to love all nature with equal passion and anyone who shares the belief in a sustainable and renewable way of life that can survive, then such are the salt of the earth, and I hope you are one of them."

"How did you come to this unshakable conviction?"

"I don't know! Perhaps it's God's answer to my prayer for forgiveness."

7

What Shall I Do?
(Ben and his dogs)

Early breakfast of home-baked bread and cheap supermarket butter washed down with a couple of mugs of Milford tea over, Dolly and Chippy (mother and son) both fed, so I blew out the candle, as the rising sun dispersed the grey dawn. My fire billowed smoke into the cabin till the chimney warmed to its task. Then all came clear on this chilly day in early March as the sun topped the hill lying to the east opposite and shone directly into my small abode.

I fanned the flames, put on a pan of last season's potatoes, then, feeling comfortable, I wondered, will I survive eighteen more months in my smoky old cabin, with no fixed income beyond casual seasonal work, such as grape-cutting and fruit-picking, plus my garden-produce off my small eco-garden of three-quarters of an acre of marginal land, until I retire?

In such moments I cast my mind back ten years to that warm fulsome May morning when I arrived in an old VW. I'd agreed to do appropriate work for the proprietors of a rambling old farm-stead. (Part of a tiny Hamlet of four homes in the South of France near the Pyrenees.)

Dotted around are vineyards, alternating with cultivated

gardens, abandoned pieces, and these interspersed with rocky outcrops running down into a steep valley with a small stream babbling its way to the vineyards on the lush fertile plain below. It is mysteriously wild and so variegated in flora and fauna, it never ceases to be attractive and full of unexpected delights for eyes, nose and ears.

What lessons can I learn from three thousand, six hundred and fifty days spent cultivating my gardens, experimenting with the powerful forces of water, sun, wind and earth, and in between, socialising with the locals, writing the odd poem, short story, etc., as inspiration comes?

Isn't life a matter of faith? I reminded myself. If faith needs proof, then it turns into science, and is no longer a belief or an act of faith.

Surely life must rest upon belief upon faith in the life-force! What about the old russet apple-tree that nearly died this year of canker? If that survives after me cutting it back so severely and grafting new shoots, if my geranium and petunia cuttings take, as well as my favourite rose 'Anabell' cuttings begin to send out shoots, I shall be filled with contentment as well as restored in faith. Will they all shoot and show faith? Not scientific certainty, nothing could be more boring, but simple affirmation of life inside.

Faith has carried me through till now, so why am I filled with vague doubts and fears this year? I wonder if it is that I still have a lingering desire for certainty, for predictability, like so many of my contemporaries? Probably so!

But, to be fair, I have to admit this winter has been a very real struggle to make ends meet, to find enough old wood to burn on my tiny fire and to earn enough money to buy food for the dogs and me.

Yes indeed. A cold old winter at the back of me, but not

much left in the kitty, low on garden produce and not much chance of work around here way out in the depths of the French south country.

Maybe I have a chance to make a couple of chairs for ecology sympathisers and make a little ready cash, then I will set to and cultivate my garden in the usual way.

Hope filled my soul and I went out immediately and sharpened chisels, plane and marking-knife, ready to start on the first chair.

What about the Arab bedouins crossing the desert to complete their pilgrimage to Mecca in order to pay their respects to Allah and Mohammed the prophet, in Saudi Arabia? Yes, remembering what others have achieved in difficult conditions helps. Incas, way up in the Andes, in South West America, building their massive temples and civic buildings with blocks of stone weighing several tons each. No modern machines: only pulleys and levers, the rest solid muscle and indomitable will, and faith in life.

Confidence – a rare quality – not to be confused with audacity, false pride, or slip-shod technical assurance: derived from study of a narrow field, the like of which is a drunkard's mirage I can tell you.

Even money based on 'scientific' theories of economics, is today buying less and less as they print more and more of this squalid 'legal tender' in most modern countries. How can I have confidence in such phony counters – mere tokens – not real wealth.

Bedouins crossing the Sahara show more savvy, bartering salt for rice, and gold for camels and horses, than the money-barons of Wall Street in New York, Bond Street in London, or in the Bundesbank in Berlin. All currencies yo-yoing continuously and dangerously measured against the American Dollar, which does the same gymnastics, in desperate attempts to balance the nation's books, and to control the uncontrollable currency pirates, now operating world-wide without scruples.

Thankfully I have abandoned such false assurance that paper money inflicts many years ago. I manage with as little of the fickle stuff as I possibly can. Instead I have come to rely upon my released ingenuity (yes, Nature teaches this) and my four stalwart friends: garden, sun, wind and water. All more reliable than paper money, but not negotiable, so I'm obliged to earn a little of the filthy lucre in order to survive.

Having cooked my potatoes I put on a few beetroots in the same water to save fuel. I looked at my two dogs and decided they are both fit. I took a comb – tidied them, then myself.

Still holding this solitary dialogue, I argued that a little of that paper money would be welcome. Dog food down, as well as my own provisions. Tea, sugar and milk, enough for one more week, a few leeks, cabbage, onions, beets, sprouts, potatoes and half a marrow.

Suddenly my seed potatoes caught my eye. They were germinating well. Scientists would say 'responding to sunlight and photosynthesis with the predictable result'. Why name a mystery? Is my response. They don't need a scientist or any other kind of certainty except their life inside. If they get caught with a late frost they take it on the chin. So I'll try to be the same, they accept their fate, come what may. I shan't try to escape mine either. I'll live out my little drama and see what happens. Those cheerful robins too! They come close for crumbs and remain happy whatever the environment.

What about resources of wholemeal flour though? About five kilos, enough for four weeks. I'll repair the coffee grinder (re-bush it) so as to grind the flour fine and so make better bread. Then I'll get on and make a chair for Catherine and maybe one for Bridget too.

Yes, that's it, get solvent again with the masquerading devil paper money. If only a little and for a short time, until garden produce permits me to barter new season's potatoes, etc., for goat's cheese, milk and eggs.

If I returned to the city of Derby in England I'd be OK for paper money, but nothing else! No sky, no cliffs, no fierce winds, no river running past my garden down into that mysterious grotto at the bottom, no chance to experiment with fresh garden produce giving me a unique chance to live as a vegetarian, and no chance to make my own electricity from wind and water for nothing, except to make the wind-charger and turbine.

Instead live in a bed-sitter, put fifty pence in the electricity meter and fifty pence in the gas meter. Collect a bottle of milk off the doorstep, letters from the box, pay the rent, pay the window-cleaner and go shopping once per week in the market. Go for a pint of insipid steel-canistered beer on Saturday night, and number five window at the labour exchange every alternate Monday morning. The rest of it, as predictable as an electronic computer. Ten pounds for rent, two-fifty for gas, two pounds sterling for electricity, leaving fifteen pounds, fifty pence for food, clothes and toilet necessities.

No, not at any price! Not for me, living like a vegetating moron in Derby or any other city in the UK. Those there can have their city certainties. I'll rest content with Nature's mysteries, right here in this little back-water of a French hamlet (Hameau) even though nothing is certain.

Dolly, my lady dog, has had twelve litters of beautiful pups, all healthy, showing supreme faith in the life-force without requiring proof other than her own *joie de vivre* and now at eleven, she's full of life and eager for another romance when she finds a likely husband.

Given these signs and portents of powerful mother Nature, I don't believe I've wasted these latter years in returning to the roots of life away from the hot furnace of city life. One ecology book typed up, a short story in the hands of a publishing agent, a few poems about Nature in competitions. Things are never as black or as good as they appear always.

If I succeed with a short story, I shall be encouraged and stimulated to continue my modest experiments in eco-living. For in so doing, others may be helped to try out their own ideas for living in harmony with all.

At present there isn't much of an eco-echo here in this hamlet after ten years. The people round about are traditional, and don't budge more than half an inch every decade. So I'll have to soldier on and hope my personal friends will enjoy visiting in the summer.

Here I am with my own electricity supply gratis from the wind and water: and small as it is, it has done good service over the years.

What if I had money though? I would make a much larger unit and have it as a multi-purpose machine – able to cut wood, grind corn, turn a washing-machine, pump water into a tower for irrigation, oxygenate stagnant water or even grind coffee. So many useful possibilities to use science imaginatively in a clean and safe manner. Yet people generally prefer centralised systems, either conventional or nuclear, and pay a big electricity bill every three months.

Well for me it is zero interest, being dangerously opposed to clean air and a safe environment. It is expensive too, especially telephone and telegraph services. I despise both and decline to use them except in dire emergencies, such as a fire hazard. There have been two serious bush fires which came close to my cabin in recent years, started by criminal arsonists who wished to burn me out. Some are jealous that I have settled here in France, and so I am still regarded as a stranger – a foreigner – except by my close friends, but not all are neighbourly – they try to make me chain my dogs even though they are gentle, and they cut off water supplies in dry periods. So I keep to myself and Nature these days. It could be different but human beings are so perverse, so nationalistic these days, one could believe there'd been no terrible war against bestial fascism. That is how it is.

Thirty-five fascists elected to the 'Chambre des deputies', in a recent national election here in France. That is how it is too.

My new won faith in life therefore springs from the examples in Nature mentioned earlier, not from people en masse, for most are cynics, competitive vampires or worse. All my cuttings, graftings and plantings give me lessons in the daily expression of faith. If they survive I'll be sublimely happy. And if my friends take delight in my gardens, dogs and eco-experiments, then my cup of joy will be brim full.

Why have I written this personal testimony, when I regard most people as cynics, misogynists, concubines and competitive miscreants? Well, lingering in the soul of each one of us, is that priceless gem of soul: of consciousness, which populations in the mass don't seem to possess. I believe this is because we are conditioned – brain-washed to accept the status-quo. We can and should throw it off. Our individual consciousness can be revived – fanned into a flaming passion for a beautiful world – a safe and clean planet with all of us living in harmony with another, if we use science to the glory of God, not for our own decadent luxury.

In my younger days I was foolish enough to expect to find my paradise in concert with humans only. Neglecting Nature and vainly trying to find my pleasure in politics, education (artificial not natural) religion (instead of natural piety) entertainment (mostly commercial) and relaxation (inside a house not in the country).

For me it was and still is a waste of time, for we are too conditioned: too interested in the narrow and fallacious certainties of pseudo science, where these disciplines are divorced from an all round vision of Universal Brother and Sisterhood.

My eleventh hour change has given me contentment, much happiness and genuine satisfaction. Need I say more in praise of natural eco-living!

My real enemies are 'humans' when only half grown pygmies rather than full statured mature people. No enmity from savage Nature – untamed, bloody and long in tooth and claw – as it is supposed to be.

Our human cruelty, both physical and psychological is far more dangerous, and much more evil than wildlife ever can be.

Let us begin to honour wildlife and in so-doing recover life as it was in the 'garden of Eden', when all had enough spiritual purity to respect all life. None being neglected or cruelly tormented in these days of so-called 'enlightened civilisations' where man is grossly over-valued and the ecosystems that support we humans seriously under-valued.

One month later, I am pleased to tell you, almost all plant graftings and cuttings have sprouted. Two chairs already sold to friends, and friendly visitors appreciate seeing simple home-made machinery producing current from wind and water.

8

A Change for the Better

Billy Beckett was a throw-back. Everybody who knew him as a boy became aware of that but from what and from where? He could never answer these questions because he wasn't aware that he was a queer fish. His parents, relatives and friends saw in him a crude vitality coupled to a delicate sensitivity which everyone thought was more appropriate to anyone living in the middle-ages or to a pastoral or even a feudal way of life when people needed such elements in their blood.

However, in a modern technocracy he wasn't at all acceptable as he was, so everyone agreed a change for the better was necessary. In his early teens his parents did their best to discipline him by sending him to the local St David's protestant church of England where he became a choirboy. They also persuaded him to join the scout-troop attached to the church, a couple of months later when it became clear that choir practice wasn't sufficient to bring about the desired changes.

Billy enjoyed the games of British-bulldog, a very rough game where half the troop fought the other half or rather engaged in mortal combat. According to whether you think getting your nose broke or your ear made into a cauliflower is a way of staying mortal or quickly becoming immortal, in this 'team-game'.

To be good at it, one had to bulldog your way through enemy lines and place a skittle or a knotted rope (whichever the scout-master preferred, according to his mood) onto the heart of the enemy territory. In order to do this one had to display those hearty bulldog characteristics: prestigious and so highly valued in British folklore and public life. British bulldog and rugby football are two forms of legalised assault that you do not have to go to prison for in England, as hearty, if dangerous, aggressiveness is valued greater than gentle tolerance.

The hall wasn't large enough and the cast-iron radiators got in the way, so there was always plenty of bloody noses and bruised limbs. But this result was better than boys going off with each other into the woods to pick flowers and recite poetry to each other, as that 'stuff' was regarded as cissy. However, the physical contact, pace and sheer fury of the 'game' plus the intense pride Billy felt when his side won, spurred him to do his best (like they do in parliament).

The lessons in self-reliance that followed such as semaphore, practiced with old red dusters fastened to sticks and Kim's game that a bloke named Rudyard Kipling invented when Kim, a young Indian boy British spy, trained himself to observe and memorise enemy positions and numbers. He did this by looking at dozens of objects and articles laid out on a cloth of gold in the Indian market place at Kabul, or sometimes near the Khyber Pass, and it confused Billy quite a lot. He knew Kim was capable of remembering many objects by name after only a few glimpses and he could name five only. Then there was the learning to tie knots of all sorts so if you tied a prisoner up he wouldn't get free unless he was a Houdini. And when you owned a big boat you'd be able to tie it to the wharf without making a laughing stock of yourself by falling off the gang-plank when you came ashore. Then there was first-aid to stop people from dying from loss of blood and then, as though all that wasn't enough to make you pretty handy, the scoutmaster wanted to see if you could light a fire outside. He gave you three matches to light a pile of old wood he'd pinched off the church-hall caretaker after sprinkling water onto it.

All these training courses were too boring for Billy but the fierce games got his blood up and he found it difficult to make it go down again, for being a queer fish his animal endowment was considerable and he revelled in touching and scragging the other boys like they do in parliament, when their blood is up.

Be that as it may, he felt that after a rough and tumble and the blood letting, these should be followed with tender considerate elements he'd learnt or began to imbibe in as a choirboy in order to help his blood to go down.

These two dissimilar influences in his life of British bulldog and being in the choir as a chorister and the gentleness of his grand-parents in Wales where they lived away from the barbaric English and the rough and tumble of school-life were fairly dominant. After all, does not a young boy gain his stature within the ranks of his peers by just such a balance between aggressive self-assertiveness and docile easy acceptance of the organs of society like schools and councils, etc. Only when these influences become fragmented and unrelated do they become dangerous to the person who swings too far to one or the other extreme. Becoming a cissy or a brute!

Billy was not naturally aggressive or docile. He tended to be, if anything, over-sensitive, which is not a good characteristic to possess in a modern technocracy, for he responded eagerly when the local parson or the choir-master asked him to sing a solo at even-song without receiving money for it. Although he was glad if a silver sixpence was thrust into his hand, as often happened. He was as good as gold when doing something for the sheer joy of doing it and that isn't a good quality to possess either, so he was up to his neck in being a queer fish when everyone else was normal and on the make all the time.

Neither did he object or cause an unholy stir when a visiting parson found him irresistible and caressed his legs under his white surplice one Sunday night as he sat in the vestry before the service began. In fact Billy found it a pleasant way of passing the time and this event filled Billy first with wonderment then astonishment and finally with intense sensations of pleasure.

This pleasant happening did not conflict in the least with his wild desire and unfulfilled ambition to do a somersault from the lamp-post cross-bar as easily as Tommy Skinner, from the end of the road, a boy who was known for his acrobatic skill and his bullying of small boys as well as for chewing gobstoppers in the front row of the choir-stalls whilst the parson was holding forth about Jesus from the pulpit. Tommy had done a blinder of a somersault one day and Billy failed so the gang shouted 'coward', tied him to a lamppost with a couple of skipping-ropes and practiced throwing tennis balls at that region so delicate to a small boy on account of the fact that a boy of Billy's age, thirteen years, is just getting to know what to do with it apart from the usual. So it was highly humiliating when one landed on it as it did that late evening.

Worse was to come though.

After one particularly wonderful Saturday night when the reverend Aldis had called for a chat and a cup of tea and stayed on to see Billy's brother Morris and then himself take a bath in front of the fire, for it was cold upstairs and, after he had enjoyed what he saw, he gave them both a new sixpenny-piece each. Saturday's joy was followed by Sunday morning which turned into a dead dull day until two friends and Billy took off to the river nearby.

There at the river, they met Tommy Skinner, Joey Alcock and Peter Bottomly. At first they seemed friendly and all bought a glass of fresh milk from Pilkington's farm. Then Billy shared his Woodbines amongst the six, whilst demanding from Tommy Skinner a kind of a ransom in the form of a sworn promise that he wouldn't ever scrag him again. They all lit up and decided to go across the golf-links and down the gully instead of crossing by the bridge like all the knobs and toffs who play golf on Sundays do.

A small stream at the bottom of the gully acted as a hazard for golfers and a haven of adventure for the lads who preferred to egg each other on to see who could jump furthest across without falling in or chickening out when they came to the widest point. It was a hot summer's day and the games ended in a scragging match when Billy tried to jump the last bit as good as Joey Alcock who grabbed an overhanging branch like Tarzan and landed real neat. Billy tried but with his crude vitality and delicate sensitivity getting all mixed up he fell in up to his 'trumper'. That's what inspired the scragging match as usual.

Every one of the group wanted to help Billy at first, by taking his shorts off and spreading same out in the boiling sun to dry. But Tommy Skinner had a pocket full of golf balls which he'd just acquired and ball bearings which he'd found on the tip. Being an ingenious technocrat in embryo, he was suddenly inspired to see if the golf balls or at least the three-quarter-inch balls would fit Billy Beckett's trumper. So with a sudden gleam of inspired inventive genius, which expressed hundreds of years of scientific know-how in one devilish gleam, he took Billy's underpants off and what with Peter Bottomly sitting on his head and Joey Alcock plonked on his legs and ankles and his mates fleeing for their lives, Tommy could experiment in peace.

His zeal to know and understand just how one thing fits another was thoroughly satisfied and Billy was freed when Joe had managed to shove a couple up and found they fitted perfectly.

Luckily Billy had an anal fixation due to his habit of eating huge platefuls of Kellogg's corn-flakes and a chieftain loaf every day and this made him subject to constipation. On his way home the ball bearings dropped out harmlessly enough and Billy kept them in a top draw for years afterwards as souvenirs of his wild boyhood.

After this humiliation Billy began to change. It was first noticeable during the constricted cricket that they enjoyed in the entry that ran the full length of the road and lay between the back-to-back rows of houses. The entry wasn't wide enough but they made do because only the toffs could afford to play properly on the field near the golf-links. So they tried to shy the ball, usually a corky, along the entry to the make-shift scrubbing-board propped up with bricks, serving as wickets, with such force, that when hit, no fielder tried to catch it.

Everyone noticed when Tommy Skinner was in that Billy Beckett always bowled the ball and one day, two weeks before bonfire night, he bowled it with such God almighty fury that it hit Tommy such a thud on his left leg, it made him dance around like an automatic wound up clockwork marionette for five minutes and the umpire definitely gave 'out' on a leg before wicket verdict.

Feuding between the two gangs reached a dangerous pitch when one week before the fifth of November found the two pinching each others' firewood and guarding their respective dens with home-made bows and arrows. First the church-end pile looked healthy enough to be called a bonfire, then suddenly it caught a fever and went ever so thin, whilst the 'co-op' one at the other end of the street fattened and mounted mysteriously during the night.

Old oilcloth floor-coverings, rolled up and looking like red Indian totem poles from Wyoming or somewhere like that. Rusty bedsteads and broken settees looking forlorn and sorry for themselves, as though they knew they weren't ever going to be slept on or sat on or made love on ever again. Such items of discarded domestic life appeared first on one pile and then on the other, causing the neighbours to doubt who to make treacle-toffee for, as they couldn't be sure which of the two gangs would celebrate the near success of Guy Fawkes who tried harder than anyone else to blow the houses of parliament up.

Mrs Rowbotham, who often gave Billy sixpence for bringing their fish and chips supper from the chippy at the corner of the park every Friday night, said that she hoped the church-end bonfire would be best, as her husband who worked at the gas-works and could shove a ten-ton coke wagon along on his tod, had saved all his football sporting chronicles for the whole year. And he refused to part with them until he was sure their end was big enough, then she'd give him the Guy she was making as well as the papers and treacle-toffee.

All passed off all right on the night, except for Harry

Perkins who lost his right thumb letting a rocket off by hand instead of from a Tetley's beer bottle and Tommy Skinner who crept up on the church-end fire and let an arrow from his bow into the crowd. It would have been not so bad if a wooden one because then it might only have been a knock-out blow. But Tommy was always looking for ball-bearings and broken umbrellas, the steel stays of which made strong lethal arrows and what's the use of a budding technocrat having anything but the best? The only problem was that this time the experimental zeal that Tommy always employed (for he'd discovered you could get away with a lot in this world if you explained to the unscientific that you were carrying out a technical experiment rather than a human one), almost produced tragic if not fatal results, for the shaft landed on Brian Moss's head and the boy nearly died.

All this was a long way back though and since then Billy had accepted the usual fights at school and in the park and the furious partisanship shown at local football matches where innocent spectators and even the referee got hurt with beer bottles and cans that people didn't know what to do with. Then there was his father's allotment to be dug over in case the Germans started another war and we had to put our backs once more into digging for victory. Then there was his morning and evening paper rounds delivered on a bike given to him by a man who took a fancy to him in the church choir and who later managed to get his name in the papers for fighting with strange men on the allotments and who later wrote a book on the theme of 'how to be happy though human' and everyone thought he'd gone mad for what has happiness and being human got to do with life in a modern technocracy?

And then Billy remembered that his kindly benefactor,

the one who gave him the only bike he'd ever had, used also to paint battle ships, as he had been in the navy on a man-o-war and this is what made him gentle and thoughtful for others, ' 'cause he didn't believe in war no more.' He turned his genius to inventing gadgets for the building and ship-building trades, some of which he patented. But before he made money from his creative ideas, police found he died mysteriously whilst the gas-oven jet was left on. With great deductive skill the police said that this painter, writer, singer sailor in HM Navy, public benefactor and inventor, had committed suicide whilst the balance of his mind was disturbed. Billy was impressed but not convinced by such police reporting. This wasn't a full or accurate account. Perhaps there had been despair, loneliness, unutterable isolation from others because he was so richly talented being an artist and not quite 'normal'. A man who positively loved people tenderly in a broad tribal sort-of-way because he wasn't possessive of materials in the same way as 'normal' people were about houses, washing-machines, wives and children.

At first Billy accepted all this as 'normal' because that's what it's all about, for this is England and everyone knew that this is the best country in the wide world to live in.

Only later, when he worked in a big factory, did he find such a vivid contrast between what he had come to recognise as the boy scout and church-choir values and way of life and those factory vulgarities that he soon became a part of but which made him think a lot deeper than usual.

At the factory he had to fight other apprentices to make sure he didn't lose his place in the queue when brewing up time came, which entailed collecting thirty cans and putting the brews in each can, placing them neatly in a large steel tray and running to the boilers.

The men didn't take kindly to one who was slow at delivering these hot beverages. Some with hard boiled eggs floating on top like bits of an afterbirth, as some opened with the quick heat.

He'd seen a real afterbirth at Mr Evans's farm in Wales but the men knew best so he never questioned their liking for eggs that floated on top of their tea or coffee, nor with the rough language employed with each other and himself sometimes.

Soon he used bad language the same as the others for no one understood if you didn't. So he changed quite a lot from a relatively innocent choirboy (who only wet the bed very seldomly in winter because he had a small bladder and yet still drank too much milk before going to bed). And he only chewed sweets in the choir stalls on Sunday evenings when most of the congregation had dozed off and his dad had gone sound asleep. He changed from that, to a pimply faced fiercely resolute brewer of tea and bringer of tools and general factotum for all and sundry.

On visiting the toilet he got interested in the graffiti and rude drawings on the sides of the green painted walls and used to hear very human noises coming from next door. He was intrigued also by the little holes bored through and curious eyes looking at his private parts. Billy supposed that they did this because the private sector was much more interesting than the public one.

He was mildly curious about all these disturbing experiences and wondered what to do. Whether to get angry or accept all as part of factory life. "Worse things happened at sea," so Frank Howarth the foreman had told him so it might be more dangerous but less boring at sea even if it was more vulgar. Boredom was Billy's mortal enemy, so when he grew up he had in mind that he might just go to sea, to see if what the foreman had said was true.

As it was, he was still an apprentice engineer and wasn't changing quick enough into a technocrat to suit his parents so he remained a queer fish in their eyes.

Albert Smart sent him across to the forge with some lathe tools that needed hardening and tempering and the smithy said he'd have them done the following morning if the boilermen didn't go out on strike and cut off his supply of steam to the steam-hammers. The next day Billy asked for them in a very vulgar way, for his crude vitality was uppermost that morning. The big burly operator clouted him from one end of the forge to the other before he found his manners and apologised. Then, when things were sorted out the smithy took him round the shoulders and said, "Billy don't become like the other cheap rubbish in this factory. I can see you're a lad of breeding and so let it stay that way. I only check lads as has a bit of good stuff in 'em. I don't waste my time on rubbish!"

This event taught Billy that there are great differences between people even in factories where they are supposed to be such bovine stereotypes. Some do try, however difficult it may be, to act as if scouts and choirs are important cultural influences and make all the difference, whilst others drift along and forget or ignore all decencies. When they accept everything as though life is just 'one God damned thing after another without distinction' as in America.

Then there was the kind lady in the dairy shop halfway along the cycle journey home, where he dropped off for a pint of milk. Who poured his milk into a glass as though it was a benediction. Then further along the same road, there was the homoeopathic doctor who watched the traffic go by from the end of his drive and had a far away look in his eyes as though dreaming of a country where everyone was healthy and he didn't need to patch people up to live in dreary towns. He was especially attentive towards Billy and always gave a cheery wave whilst looking searchingly at his legs as he returned a salutation. Billy decided he wasn't the only person who regarded boredom as the world's deadly enemy.

It isn't easy to pin-point exactly the particular event or experience that resulted in Billy changing his style of life and swinging over by slow degrees from the rough coarse aggressive and vulgar to the gentle receptive conciliatory and even humble vagabond that he later became. But no doubt it was a contrast of happenings somewhere between the ball bearing experiment on his tender trumper which didn't upset him all that much, followed by incidents related above. Plus his frequent holidays in Wales, where he learned to shoot rabbits, pick strawberries and visit beautiful gardens and flower-shows with his frail old grandfather. And he weighed tomatoes and filleted fish in his uncle's green-grocery shop, where the sharp-eyed Welsh shoppers already loaded to the gunnels, made complimentary remarks when he gave good weight as he often did. And who scolded him unmercifully when he was a mite under or when he dropped fruits on the floor whilst trying to swing the paper-bags as expertly as his uncle could, who was often busy cleaning or harnessing Dolly up to the cart ready for the round. He'd tear him off a strip as well and in front of Mrs Davis the ladies hair-dresser from next door, who used to make eyes at him when she wasn't putting the hair-dryer onto someone's head, or looking at Jacky Roberts the handsome milkman who often dropped in for a yarn about the gee-gees with his uncle Albert.

Anyhow, somewhere along the busy thoroughfare of life's amazing voyage, gentleness prevailed and he became a disciple of the great champion of and architect of India's freedom, the one and only Mahatma Gandhi. Everyone knows he liberated five hundred and fifty million Indians from the clutches of the British Colonialists, simply by holding up a flower one prayer time in nineteen-forty-two. The year of independence came soon after the war when Gandhi started a policy of non-cooperation with civil authorities. He asked his followers to boil water from the sea and so provide their own salt, rather than pay tax on it from the shops, before Gandhi's campaign began.

Billy was convinced that this method was less boring than buying salt, and helped everyone to get their crude vitality and delicate sensitivity into complete harmony.

9

Oliver's Trip

Ten year old Oliver lives in Bristol with his dad Len and mum Doris. His dad studies at university and mum teaches at a local school.

One day Oliver heard a mystery voice ask, "Who are you?"

Oliver didn't wish to be rude so he said, "I'm Oliver Leemas."

"That only tells me your name. I want to know lots of things, such as, how tall you are? What you like to eat? What games you play? Where have you been? So as I can really be your mate when you're fed up with school or TV or when the cat scratches your leg and makes you angry. Will you be my pal?"

"Well I'll think about it! You are quite a gentle voice so probably I will tomorrow, if you turn up?"

"Oh, you can be sure I'll be near, just like a pet dog, or hamster or whatever pet you have. All you have to do, is be quiet on your own in a wood, forest, room or mountain and, like a willing slave, but more as a friend, I'll come and cheer you up. And when everything is going fine, well, we can

169

h

share that too.

"But first I want to hear your voice, so as to tell you from all the others. You can tell me about last year's holiday in France please."

"Well, Mr Voice, I like to go to Avonmouth with my dad and mum to watch the boats come in loaded with fish for Bristol market and one day, after we had fish and chips for supper, I asked my father to take us across the channel to France for our summer holidays." He stopped telling his story and asked Mr Voice a question. "Are you full, have you had your dinner? And do you like playing near rivers and climbing trees in the sunshine?"

"Yes of course, I've had soup and bread and yes, I will always come to you when out in the country playing, so you won't ever be lonely. But now please tell me your story. It is quite interesting and I don't know about France." And that is all Oliver remembered before falling asleep.

Sure enough his new pal, Mr voice, was there sitting on a chair near the window patiently waiting for him to wake up.

"Come and sit on the bed near me Voicy, and I'll explain all about my trip to France."

"I'm ready, but hadn't you better have your breakfast first Olly?"

"No, Mum and Dad are still asleep and it's Sunday, so they have a sleep-in. We have a late breakfast Sundays, but thanks all the same. You've had your breakfast I suppose so now I'll tell you, just the best bits. You'll have to imagine the rest."

"You went in your father's van I take it?"

"Ten hours travel and we arrived in Calais, crossed from Dover in a ferry: 'The Spirit of Free Enterprise'. Quite fun really because, after exploring, I met Tommy on B Deck winning money from the fruit-machines. He gave me tenpence, I tried and lost so we both went up to the boat-deck, whilst Mum and Dad had a drink in the saloon.

Seagulls swooping down to catch fish churned up in the ship's wake, then the clouds lifted and we saw France for the first time.

Then, just as we were counting all the birds, and looking at their big fat grey breasts and strong wings and yellow eyes, a tall man dressed in a uniform with brass buttons and yellow stuff round his peaked cap, asked us what we were doing? I was just about to say 'Just looking around the ship' but Tommy chirped up, 'Oh we're waiting for the captain to show us how to steer the ship.' 'Come with me to the bridge,' the captain said, so we climbed the small gangway into the bridge and wheel-house where the first mate was guiding the ship's rudder to left or right."

"Why Olly, why to left or right?"

"Well you see Voicy, it's the currents and waves, sometimes due to wind and at others the moon's gravity – full moon pulls the water, causing high and low tides, and there's the Gulf-stream too, so the captain explained about the compass, you know, three hundred and sixty degrees; north, south, east, west. I noticed we were going roughly SSE to Calais. He said it's set in gimbals so it doesn't shake and shudder with the engines and the roll of the ship. By this time we were well out and he telegraphed below for 'full speed', as there weren't any more small fishing-boats in view. He pulled a lever above a dial showing stop, slow ahead half, full ahead, etc. Sonar, radar, and all the other gadgets too. But I guess the engineer didn't hear the telegraph bell because nothing happened for a couple of minutes, but then it did, maybe he was reading or drinking tea.

"Then Tommy wanted to climb to the top of the funnel to

get a better view. The captain said, 'Now you young lads return to your parents, as we are due in the port of Calais in fifteen minutes.'

"Calais was bright and sunny and we got through customs with no bother, then Dad started driving on the right and I thought he'd gone crazy, but Tommy's dad was doing the same, and then my dad told me, that's the law, in France. It felt funny but we soon got used to it. Big sharp-pointed buildings like church-steeples, castles, shops, then we stopped at a café called 'Marie Suzanne' for tea-time. Sat under these big elms, big leaves, plenty of shade, clean tables outside. I'd seen Tom go by scudding off in their car down south. I felt sad to lose him, but soon the waiter arrived, after my dad said, 'garcon, s'il vous plait', and served us with drinks. Whilst drinking a Pepsi, I had time to look around. Close by bare-chested boys and men played boule with heavy steel balls, shouted and clapped when one landed near the pilot. Others walked elegantly with girl-friends, shirts draped over their bums, almost covering their shorts so I asked mum and she said, 'Yes Oliver, take your shirt off if you like to get brown just like these French people,' so I did.

"Then we paid up and set off once again in the boring old van. We came to a road-sign, white with blue letters, saying 'Calais' struck through with a red mark to show the end of the town. Then a park and lovely trees and a mother pulling a little boy's velvet shorts up after he'd had a little pee. Well Voicy, I thought how natural everything is in France. Tell you the truth, I'd already forgotten about Bristol and our house, I really began to feel just a bit French. You won't split will you?"

"No, no Olly, never a whisper about your private remarks. I must say it all makes a 'rare story'. Didn't you get sea-sick or travel-sick, ever?"

"No, but when I grow up I'll travel everywhere on a bike, because it keeps you fit and you see everything and you don't ever get sick or headaches even.

"So now we went through wide open country . . . miles of Indian corn, sugar-beet, wheat and a big elm tree every fifty metres. Boy-o-boy it was shady! After two hours, dad stopped at a campsite. Mum was tired, Dad had had enough driving, we had our first French meal in the camp restaurant.

"I felt hungry too but not tired so Dad said I could have a quick dip in the pool, shaped like a dolphin, then join them at table three. It didn't work out because I met some friends and we raced each other and I couldn't stop laughing when they tried to speak English and they laughed when I tried French. So sandwiches and a glass of milk on the patio, still in my trunks, whilst my parents had coffee near the pool. Being a warm night and the pool being floodlit underneath, many campers showed off how well they could dive. There were some real swank-pots, all oiled up and looking as though they'd spent months on the beach. Dad came, climbed to the top board, looking ever so pale, but did a beauty from the spring-board."

"Well Olly, I must say you do look healthy and brown since you returned, but tell me, did you see any dead trees? I've heard so many stories about fires and acid rain, (that's sulphuric acid from car-exhausts and chimneys) killing trees?"

"Yes, sad to say, when we passed through Geneva and on the way to Mont Blanc, which you can see sticking up about five thousand metres, going south, we saw big blackened hills and gorges where fires were. About the others? No, can't say I did, but we met an old Englishman in the south, living in a small cabin, who told us about fish dying from poisoned paint put on ships to stop sea-life clinging to the hull and he said some trees were dead or dying near him, because all the leaves curled up and new shoots were trying to grow from the bottom of each tree, making a last effort."

"Do you believe in God Olly? I mean going all that way in the family van with your dad and mum. Didn't you have any scary moments?"

"Now you mention it Voicy, at that first camping place and after swimming, we went to bed and the moon was shining onto my bed at the front and I heard a night-owl hooting down near the river. I really thought 'this is heaven!' Then Mum drew the curtains and I don't remember anything else. But Dad said someone tried to open the van door, about twelve-thirty, and he got up and chased a man out of the campsite.

"On the fourth night and after passing through Provence and along the Cote d'Azure – the Riviera – full of rich people and all the bays and harbours full of posh sailing yachts, we came to a town named Avignon. A fine big castle stood above the town. Great ramparts and turrets for archers and high towers for good defence against the enemy. My mum Doris, said that hundreds of years ago this castle was known as the 'Palace of the Pope'. She said that the French wanted their own Pope. You know Voicy, a kind of religious leader over all the others, because not everyone could read the Bible for themselves in those days.

"My dad Leonard said, 'Religion is very tricky, it's like cooking chips.' We looked round this big 'Palace' and I thought it was very big for even a Pope, or whatever they call him, Dad said that he had a lot of cooks and bakers and soldiers and horse-cavalry, as well as choirboys, priests, cardinals, and someone to clean his shoes and wash his hankies, that's why it was built so big.

"And a cold steel chain and manacle round the leg of anyone who didn't believe in the way the Pope cooked the panful of religion – in the dungeons with him."

"Didn't anyone take you to see the torture-chamber and dungeons, Olly?"

"Yes it was horribly cruel what they did to Protestants or Muslims, but now Dad says that everyone thinks for themselves about religion, at least in Europe but not in the Arab countries."

"Well, you tell me the French are good cooks so I suppose they can cook religion and come up with a nice dish to suit themselves."

"Voicy, that's quite a funny way to put it but I get your meaning. If you make too many mistakes judging anything, especially cooking, it's likely to come out like a dog's dinner."

"Quite right Olly! Where did you go next?"

"Next day proved to be even hotter than before so we started out of Avignon quite early. In the evening, after winding mountain roads, many vineyards, two or three big cities, we arrived at our friend's in a little cottage near the village of Brassac. It was early evening, so I took 'Ginger' the dog down to the river, climbed trees, lay in the grass and watched small fish – I think they were trout – threw sticks for Ginger and found a strong mountain-ash branch to make a bow. Then they called us in for supper. Guess what we had for supper Voicy? Well I'll tell you. We had a mountain of French fries, salad and lots of small fresh trout, deep fried. Oh boy, they were tasty."

"Wish I'd been with you on your trip."

"Well it wasn't all fun 'cause Mum made me wash up at each campsite. Then, when I had to leave Ginger, I cried and Dad told me off for being soppy. Then Mum told him off for telling me off, so I felt really down."

"I bet Ginger cried too, so you weren't the only one. You just have to take these things on the chin. Maybe you'll be down there playing in the woods with him again, next year."

"Dad cheered me up though. He suggested a dip in the sea, so after 'Bye byes' to our friends we set off. On the way we met this old man I spoke of earlier who was on about dead trees. My Dad stopped for a tyre-pressure check because of the hot roads and there was this man at the same garage. He seemed pleased to meet us and speak English for a change 'cause he's been there years, so we said we'd call at his place after our swim in the sea at Narbonne beach. Big breakers and a bit windy but miles and miles of sands and so we did what the others did, swam naked. It was very salty and Dad threw the ball at me. It splashed water into my eyes and I swallowed some when another boy, nearby, tried to duck me. But it was great. We had a picnic after, then set off.

"Eight-thirty the same day and we arrived at Geoff's cabin. It was off the main road and there was such a lovely sun shining on the little country roads, all green and golden honey-coloured wheat and very green bushes all in lines, which were grape-vines. Dad nearly knocked a chicken off for our supper, as we drove past a lonely farm, then we stopped a huge girl on a moped to ask the way. Mum's good at French and so the girl pointed straight ahead and at last we came to the end of the village and on to a twisty turny one-track road to a little hamlet (hameau) and then a little bald man in shorts only, told us how to get to Geoff's.

"There it was, in a little pocket of the valley, next to a semicircular cliff-face, looking south. Dad peeped and he came out of his tiny house and waved. I ran down the goat-track, then Dolly, his dog, came out barking. But her tail was wagging so I knew she was friendly. There he was with a beard and only trunks. We looked at each other, not knowing what to say. But without words we both knew we would be friends. He said, 'Watch the steps, it's a bit like climbing trees,' and so it was. He'd made everything except the tiny cave out of off-cuts from big trees, even a wheel-barrow and a shed where he bakes his bread. Just the opposite to the Pope's palace at Avignon and a lot more fun. It really is a 'joke house'. He lives just the opposite to everyone in towns and big palaces. Gets water from a little stream, bathes in the river, grows pure food in his gardens and gets electricity from the wind turning his wind-charger. But he'd only just come back to his cabin from the UK so no electricity, but it's light till ten, so we used candles just near the end. I wanted to explore inside the tiny cave but the back was bricked up as it led down to a big underground grotto. Nobody knew about how deep it was, and some people say it leads right down a thousand metres to the river Brian below which runs through Minervois.

"He made tea in an old pot and it began to go dark and real spooky. Bats were beginning their usual search for a tasty mouse or two and Dolly begged for a bit of my biscuit and gave me a lick and Geoff lit candles as we chatted about birds and fish and how best to be a 'friend of the earth' and all the little animals. Then Mum heard a little scratching noise at the back. 'Probably a bird or a badger or even a mouse,' Geoff offered. 'There's plenty of wildlife round here, including wild pigs, when I'm not here,' he said."

"What an adventurous holiday you had Olly! Wish I'd been with you all. And so you hope to go again next year, do you?"

"Oh rather, perhaps my dad will do the same thing one day."

"Now Olly, I have to say 'bye-bye' to you just for now and I think it is time to get up and have your breakfast. I can hear your mum cooking the bacon . . . Cheerio."

"See you soon, Voicy."

10

George the Parrot Priest

I woke early, scratched myself then scraped my beak against the bronze roosting-rod eight inches below my perch, like a tired old bishop surveying his congregation. With delicate strokes I rubbed the sleep from my eyes with my wicked left claw, whilst balancing on my right. I pruned my beautiful tail-fan plumage of deep scarlet receding to vermillion, then grey-pink at my ruff, giving an elegant taste for those who see my black curved beak and my light green pupils surrounded by white irises. I'm a natural priest, an uncrowned monarch!

Having made myself respectable once again, I settle upright and think: What will today bring? Loud vulgar jukebox music? More noisy two-legged beasts prodding and insisting I mimic their wolf-whistles, cats miaowing and rude phrases, etc.

Endurance, patience, fortitude in short the will to preserve my dignity and sanity in a crazy world. Just let one of those poke me today and I'll give them a piece of my mouth which, as you know, is a hard black beak that can crack nuts easily, so they'd better mind their manners.

Here is Marcelle fondling me and she gives me cashew nuts and a few cherries for my ageing digestion and fresh water after cleaning my dropping-board. She's so good, I like her the best. She doesn't expect me to chatter all day, like the clients. I'm here to entertain. This perch is better than my cage I was forced into five years ago. No space to fly, no shade from the sun there, where I used to languish on the centre boulevard, Ramblas, in Barcelona. So cramped sharing with Sam and Sally. And those African monkeys next door threw banana-skins into our cage, until one day I bit Adolf's fingers as he withdrew. I fight my corner always!

So many changes in life . . . not that I mind doing my stuff mimicking humans, although it is difficult explaining why to my feathered friends who think it is treacherous and undignified. Well, I say, one has to be adaptable in order to survive these days, but they insist I'm just like Frank Sinatra on an ego-trip 'doing it my way'.

They don't know me! They can't see the funny side. They ought to realise: I never imitate or mimic exactly, that's too boring for worlds in heaven or hell. So I vary my musical and vocal repertoire to suit myself and to preserve a modicum of dignity. I mean what would happen to me, for instance, if I caught a sore throat from a client? No social insurance benefit for an ageing voiceless parrot, so I'd be on the road once more, or even worse the proprietor may silence me forever!

This being the case, as I see it, it is prudent to perform only after I've tucked my head under and had a little siesta until three or four o'clock, and then only for the kindly ones who give me a few chips or a bit of bacon fat to vary my diet a little.

You see my name is George . . . 'King George' really, but these humans don't recognise royal blood! They are so boringly the same except for Marcelle. She knows I'm the most attractive member of the staff. I admire these hard-working waitresses who, like myself, make the clients comfortable and welcome whilst they eat in this town of Sète, a fishing port in the south of France. They expect immediate attention, fussing where to sit, what to eat and drink? So, if Marcelle and Nicole are overwhelmed, I begin a few wolf-whistles, then 'merci beaucoup', mimicking an old skipper who comes in every Friday night for a fish supper then escorts Marcelle home just before my roosting-time. He has a voice of thunder, so when I manage it the clients are impressed, then a sparkling recitation of dogs barking, cats miaowing, male whistles, etc. This tactic enables the girls to catch up and bring the soup before they all become bored. Surprising how easily people are bored these days. Perhaps because they lead useless unnatural lives of conformity in a trap of their own making?

Who am I to talk! Getting caught away from my natural home in the African forest. Life is hardly worth it, so I do the best I can. Anyway, I observe all from my royal throne and I use my dignity and colourful charm to obtain respect and attention from those who enter. And, as a natural priestly king, I expect strict observance of protocol. If anyone gets above him/herself, or off the line of duty, I swear profusely. My beak thrusts forwards menacingly ready to bite a finger off the one who dares to poke or ruffle my plumage.

What a lot of stupid humans, I decide, as Marcelle opens the door and approaches. I stretch my right claw elegantly for her to stroke sensitively. Oh yes! She knows how to treat a monarch. I bend over gently and take her index finger and give it a love-bite nip at the base of her nail. Marcelle recognises it as an intimate reassurance which even her boyfriend hasn't tried. She is electrified as though ancient secret forces of nature are surging from my beak. I smile mischievously, for I know I'm nature's high-priest, restoring those who are missing their natural roots by city-life and city-living.

So many clients are crude and try to humiliate me saying rude phrases and ignorant noises . . . no refinement whatsoever! These strange animals, who eat such a lot and walk upright on two long legs, with their feet encased in leather or plastic shoes, and who exhibit dangerous habits with their fingers. I can defend myself though, nature has seen to that.

After all I deserve respect. I am not to be won cheaply or easily. I'm friendly and courteous to all who approach but only give my heart to those of equal dignity and self-possession. I hope I'll be fortunate to meet a lady, a queen, as I feel lonely as a king without a soul-mate with whom to converse on equal terms. And don't forget, I bring prosperity to this restaurant.

There's Nicole serving coffee and croissants to the customers at the bar. She's so religious pouring coffee, wine or whatever, more delicately than a bishop conducting high mass. And now, more 'top-ten' hits from the juke-box, "Get closer to nature. Love me for ever. And don't let me go, etc."

What a lot of maudlin sentimentality! These humans don't know how to treat animals and precious birds like me or Adolf, the monkey I told you of. How can they appreciate each other? They need us. We show natural talent and how to bestow charms with restraint and a little dignity. That's my ambition today . . . to show what dignity really is.

Twelve o'clock, time for a little lunch and then a siesta till three, when I chirp up and let go with a long low 'wolf-whistle'; 'pretty polly'; 'leave me alone you dirty old man';

'I'm coming, said the bishop to the virgin', etc, all in French of course.

At about eight-thirty the restaurant is very busy and I'm entertaining really hard, when in comes an elegant lady: fine side-profile, hair swept up and under a wide floppy summer hat and frock to match just below her knees, accompanied by a few assorted friends. She sat below me but not under, if you follow my drift, so she could see me and everyone else. After seating them she took more interest in me than her companions. A customer passed and stroked my foot sensitively enough . . . better than being ignored. But I want the queen's attention. Yes, I recognise her as my equal . . . strong vibrations. I am determined to seduce her into paying court.

I somersault to the upside down position and begin, "Pieces of eight, pieces of eight, I'll swear like a trooper if you stay too late," in French, of course. French never ever stop eating or talking and arguing until Jean-Luc closes up. She looks up from her plate. I've aroused her curiosity, with a bit of luck she'll pay court. It's easy to be indifferent to the flotsam and jetsam; but with a 'special person' I find I like to show off all my mimicking skills. After all, protocol cuts both ways. Kings and Queens always enjoy equal courtesies and dignity. Ah, her ambassador approaches! So tedious these protocol flunkies! I survive his scrutiny and he touches me delicately. I give him appropriate signs, and hook my claws onto his outstretched finger. His finger bends under my weight, but he carries me to my royal visitor. Immediately she accepts me into her heart. Feeds me a few tit-bits of bread dipped in honey, then a few cashews and cherries. My thin brass-dipped chain, drags across her table until we are face to face. She strokes my feet warmly and now, yes, she offers her strong index finger. She's no delicate flower from a palace conservatory, she's a wild orchid 'queen of nature', who doesn't need courts, thrones or flunkies.

I take her proffered finger solemnly. At last with my equal! No need to prostitute myself playing to the gallery. Another dimension entirely . . . our eyes . . . our body language says all. I nip her finger gently. She caresses me all over, then I climb onto her left shoulder and stroke her pretty head and ear. We are one, at last. So good to know this is how close birds and humans can communicate. Sharing our loneliness, our dignity, as two originals in a brutal world. Suddenly, the old seaman André came in: shouted to Marcelle to bring his supper. Then he grabbed me off the queen's shoulder, flinging me up: which dragged the chain removing her hat and false wig. I flapped onto my perch, all dreams shattered!

11

The Acrobat from Mauritius

(Written aboard ship when Geoff Broady
was 24 years old in 1946)

One thousand miles of Indian Ocean separates the magical island of Mauritius from that lovely sea coast city of Durban in South Africa. One day in July 1946 the *Franconia* (a twenty thousand ton pleasure steamer chartered by the British government from the Cunard Company for war service) steamed from the port of Durban, and three days later nosed her way gently but steadily into the small port of St Louis on the southern tip of the island of Mauritius. She was soon safely anchored for'ard, and secured with hawsers running from her stern to buoys anchored by strong chains not far from the landing stage. Our ship could not use the stage because of her exceptional draught which was 32 feet.

Once again this twenty-three-year-old ship had brought me close to mystery and adventure which I never dreamt would come my way. Mystery because here in the middle of the Indian Ocean an island looms up on the horizon which later proves to be historically interesting, and romantically captivating because of its tropical climate, azure waters, clear skies and coral reefed bays, with palm trees fringing the edge of clean white sand.

What a white man's paradise when compared with a Manchester fog or a Liverpool dock-road with its dirty 'fish and chip' shops and evil looking pubs. The old ship brought me adventure at the same time, because I was later destined to meet a man from this island who has had a profound influence upon my life.

The ship's motorboats were lowered to help transport the mail and passengers ashore, but the really heavy luggage and cargo was handled by tenders that chugged out from the island. Aboard were a number of officials to greet us.

We were all anxious to get ashore, because the view of the island from our ship promised well for sight-seeing and swimming. Rather wistfully I was watching the privileged mail-bags and the few important passengers going off in one of the painters. Dreamily I thought about home, then letters, and so to these ordinary looking mail-bags. Exercising one's imagination may be unimportant in the great scheme of things, but one thing is certain, it fills in time. I got musing about these letters and stores going ashore to the white settlers and planters because already I had had illuminating experiences about the habits of white empire builders in such places as Mombasa and Durban. I imagined that quite a few of those innocent looking crates coming out of the bowels of the ship were full of Pilsner lager in tins, Scotch whisky in bottles, and among the barrels and boxes many kinds of wine, cheese, butter, cigarettes and cigars. Amenities which are absolutely essential out there.

About the mail, my fancy waxed more capricious because I felt quite sure that many of those letters contained in those bags would be in English and anything English makes me feel a bit capricious. I imagined the scrupulously square placed stamps on the carefully addressed envelopes. Yes,

English right to the last full stop and the inevitable, although polite, 'yours truly'. English letters expressing English thoughts produced by over intellectualised yet under nourished English nervous systems, reacting to English experiences. Oh, the thickened arteries of English men, how is it possible for us to be so insular so uncompromisingly English.

However, the French speaking shipping authorities were quite different from the planters on the island. They always greeted a big ship in a most polite way. Perhaps their courtesy is a direct result of French occupation for such a long time. A wireless message is received asking for as many officers as can be spared to come ashore for a motor-tour of the island, with a slap-up lunch and a bathing expedition in a blue lagoon, with coral reef and palm trees at the end of it. What an invitation, only one flaw, there were too many servants ready to regale you with wine or food at the midday lunch. It was a day of contrast though, because the island had recently suffered a hurricane which had almost flattened the sugar canes, and destroyed many native huts made by the people who harvest the sugar. These people are mostly of Indian origin due to the very old slave trade that once prospered out there. They were mostly French speaking but a few spoke English as well, especially those young men who had joined the British army.

Roughly two thousand pioneer troops came aboard the following day, and with eager faces and light hearts (for they were mostly young men) explored the ship in so far as their confined quarters would allow them. At sea the next day, whilst on the four to eight watch I was mystified by an almost overpowering smell emanating from the fo'c'sle of the ship. I discovered the troops busy cooking their first substantial meal of curried rice and vegetables and chapattis: a sort of unleavened bread cooked quickly in oil and spiced rather too much for my taste.

There was one man among them who was destined to teach me one of the most important lessons of my life. One can only talk about friendship subjectively for so much depends upon what imaginatively the mystery of another person's life means to one in personal terms, therefore my views about my friend are personal and consist largely of private impressions publicly expressed in this article. He was a splendid physical specimen of manhood of about twenty-eight years. Already he had won outright the championship in acrobatics for the whole of the islands of Madagascar and Mauritius. In the cool of the evening he entertained his pals with rope-tricks and agile physical feats. Singing and dancing was also popular, but reading the Bible was also an important activity for some during the day whilst they relaxed under canvas awnings.

Jim was a simple deliberate fellow with deep toned muscular voice. It was a voice I have never heard either before or since because of its warmth, friendliness and strength. He wanted me to learn French, but I was slow and did not respond to his effort as I ought to have done. We spoke English and enjoyed many long conversations.

Little did I realise how much James Valayden loved me then, for it is only now after meeting many people of different countries that one can estimate the value and intensity of feeling that one man communicates to another in friendship. He was a man who admired others rather than expecting to be admired for he was very modest about his skill and preferred to give rather than take. This was a great lesson for me in the university of life.

James, together with his compatriots, disembarked at Port Said to give the soldiers who fell at El Alamein a decent burial. What a pity we are all too English in this matter of friendship!

Yes, this contingent of young soldiers – part of the British army – had joined up, not because they were endowed with the belligerent war-gene, but because a hurricane had smashed their houses and flattened their sugar-cane crops and services of electricity. So they had come from this tiny island, sited between the mainland port of Mombasa, on the coast of Kenya, and the large island of Madagascar.

This cheerful army waved to the ship's company, as they strode down the gangway onto dry land – and each young soldier was left to ponder at leaving their beautiful island home: but so vulnerable to 'Tsunami' type hurricanes. A first trip for most! And then to face a sombre task of burying the dead British, Colonials, and German troops, who died in that tremendous battle for El Alamein: where Sir Bernard Law Montgomery trained his eighth army of Desert Rats to fight Rommel's army in the fight of their lives.

This decisive battle drove Rommel's troops and tanks to surrender at El Alamein, where many Tommies lost their lives, and thousands of Germans were killed or taken prisoner: All to be given a proper burial by those young soldiers. An experience that will remain with them as contrasting their pastoral country-life with the grim realities of humans at war, and of course, with hurricane force: a level of life they were familiar with.

So, as I stood on my 'twelve to four' watch – making sure the derricks lowered army-supplies safely onto waiting lorries, I felt lost and uneasy as to my own future on this turbulent planet.

"Take that beard off," the chief engineer commanded, when I was summoned to his cabin, half way through the Suez Canal. "And no fraternising with passengers, whether army or civilian personnel," he barked.

This reprimand translated into an uncomfortable future as a fifth-engineer aboard SS *Franconia*. Not much success for a twenty-four-year-old junior engineer, but then again that contrast between the positive colours and inspiration of James' leadership, resulting in the comradeship woven into those he led, stood out against the barbaric dismissal of any sign of friendship by a drink-sodden chief, and stuck in my memory as a lesson in friendliness between all peoples: still to be realised, struggled for, and hopefully secured, in some future heaven on earth. But whilst burying the dead in decent graves in Tunisia, observant youngsters from a tiny island named Mauritius may wonder at the unsavoury decision made by top brass in Whitehall to recruit untried soldiers to do these gruesome tasks. They will see this as dereliction of duty in failing to bury our own nationals and Germans, fallen in a battle they couldn't avoid whilst Hitler's dictatorship continued.

We need to heed these lessons as we continue aggressive adventures in Iraq and Afghanistan, in present wars, if ever we are to advance beyond the primitive concept of 'remaining above ground' at any price to life and limb, and the sustainability of this beautiful planet!

PS: May I dream that Charles Baudelaire's poems, on the perennial theme of 'evil' eventually giving to the perfumes of forgiveness and absolution when confessions are honestly put, will happen to many of the characters as well as my own in these stories submitted.